|| Jai Siya Ram ||

FRAGRANCE OF US

Touching Her Skin and Cracking Her Soul

POORNIMA SINGH

INDIA · SINGAPORE · MALAYSIA

ISBN 979-8-89724-506-2

Contents

Acknowledgement

I would like to dedicate this book to the two most incredible women in my life my mother and my sister. Your unwavering love, strength, and support have shaped who I am today. To my mother, thank you for always being my guiding light, and or showing me what true resilience and compassion look like. Your nurturing spirit is the heart of every word written in this book. To my sister, your constant belief in me, and the bond we share, have helped me through my darkest days and brightest moments. I could not have made it this far without both of you.

A heartfelt thank you to my father and my younger brother. Papa, your wisdom and encouragement have always pushed me to strive for greatness. Thank you for believing in me even when I doubted myself. To my younger brother, your laughter and love have been a constant source of joy and inspiration. I am forever grateful for both of you.

I must also extend my deepest thanks to my dear friends Dilip, Pragati and Prerna. Your friendship has been a haven for me. You both have stood by my side, offered wisdom, and reminded me of the power of true, unconditional friendship. I am so lucky to have you both in my life.

A very special thanks to Rishabh, whose unwavering belief in me has been a constant source of strength. Your encouragement has illuminated this journey in ways I cannot fully express. Your faith in my potential, even when I struggled to see it in myself, has been a beacon that kept me going. I am deeply grateful for your support and friendship.

To all of you, this book would not have been possible without your love, encouragement, and steadfast support. Thank you for being my rock throughout this journey.

Preface

'Fragrance of us' is a journey through love, loss, and healing. It tells the story of a woman who navigates the complexities of a broken relationship, confronting her own insecurities and fears. When love fades and trust is shattered, how do we rebuild? Can we heal when the one we love slips away?

This tale is not just about romantic love, it's about discovering inner strength, forgiveness, and the realization that sometimes, the most profound healing comes from within. *Aadhvita* captures the essence of heartache and growth, offering a reflection of our struggles and triumphs.

As you read, I invite you to find pieces of your own story in these pages. It's a tale of resilience, courage, and hope reminding us that even in our most fragile moments, there's a chance for renewal. Will the past truly let go? Or will the heart always carry its scars?

'Something is not meant to be healed as the memories of it is forever pierced and within you it remained sealed'

One

A Worthful Trauma

———•◆•———

It was a chilled winter, the season of love, when the sky was veiled in fog and a delicate mist covered the windows of my small apartment. The walls, painted in shades of blue and white, made the space feel both expansive and inviting a place where one could easily linger longer than intended, though it was only rented. I sat on my comfortable grey sofa, a shade that mirrored the obsession I felt for these deep, sombre colours.

I strained to peer through the window, hoping for a glimpse of the outside world, when a voice called my name from behind, louder than usual, yet not entirely disturbing. The moment felt like déjà vu.

"Aadhvita, hey! Aadhvita, why aren't you saying something?" His voice was warm, but his eyes, those deep oceans that always drew me in held an intensity that took my breath away. His hands, cold against my skin, traced the curves of my cheeks with long, tender fingers, and his smile, as bright as ever, brought me a peace I hadn't known I needed.

"Let's go out for a drive?" he asked, excitement lacing his voice.

Surprised, I sought confirmation. "But it's raining out there!"

He looked at me, puzzled. "What? Don't you love the rain?"

"Yes, I do," I replied, my heart warming to the idea.

"Then we're going," he declared with a firmness that left no room for argument. His voice held a power over me, one that wasn't dominating but rather gently persuasive. It was impossible to deny him, even if I had wanted to. His happiness and the simple fact that he was mine made me willing to do anything for him.

"Get ready!" he shouted as he headed to the bedroom. I stood there, still in my white pullover and grey pants, with my hair tied in a lazy bun and white sneakers on my feet. I must have looked like a mess. But then, the door opened, and he stepped out. Time seemed to freeze as I took in his appearance.

"Oops," the word slipped out before I could stop it. He was a vision of perfection, as always. His eyes locked onto mine, his face flawlessly groomed, with wet hair adding to his allure. The blue jeans and white hoodie made him look irresistibly cute Mr. Tall Dhruva. Yes, that was his name.

Tall enough to turn heads, with buttery smooth skin and lips that were too pink, too perfect, sending shivers down my spine and electrifying my veins.

He stood before me with a knowing smirk as I remained lost in him. Clearing his throat, he pulled me back to reality. "Done checking me out, baby?"

"Nothing like that," I replied quickly, looking away to hide my embarrassment.

He stepped closer, his hands gently wrapping around my waist. I could smell the minty fragrance I was so obsessed with. We were so close that his lips brushed against mine, his breath mingling with my own. His grip tightened, and his lips found mine, leaving them wet with desire. I placed my hands on his cheeks and kissed him back, harder, letting the passion consume us both. He lifted me and carried me to the sofa. We fell onto it together, but nothing could stop him. His eyes were closed in pleasure, his soft lips still fervently seeking mine. At that moment, all I could think was that I was his, and he was mine.

"Aadhvita, I love you," Dhruva whispered into my ear before kissing my forehead and resting his head against my chest.

"Are you alright, Dhruva?" I asked, sensing a change in him.

"Yeah," he replied, standing up and lifting me with him. "Let's go out and enjoy the rain."

"No, I don't want to go anywhere," I admitted, feeling too weak to move from the warmth of our home.

He went to the balcony and opened the door, inviting me outside without hesitation. I ran to the open space, standing still as Dhruva followed, his arms wide open, offering me a warm embrace. I quickly wrapped myself around him, his warmth the only comfort I needed.

My heart whispered against his chest, "Can you be mine forever?" Tears welled up in my eyes, escaping before I could stop them.

He looked at me with sympathy, his voice gentle, "I'm yours already." But then his phone rang, and he pulled away, stepping inside to take the call. The moment shattered, leaving me feeling ignored and embarrassed. I was curious who was on the other end of that call that made him shrug me off so easily?

When he returned, his face was dull. "I'm sorry," he apologized softly. "I have to go back to Bangalore; it's urgent."

I was stunned, barely processing his words. "Whose call was that? What happened suddenly? You came here for a week off to spend time with me. What happened to our plans?"

"It was Vikrant," he explained. "Some clients are coming from abroad the day after tomorrow, and my boss wants me to attend to them for the company's benefit.

This is an opportunity I can't afford to miss. I hope you understand."

I nodded, though my mind struggled to grasp what was happening.

"Thanks, baby!" He stepped closer, planting a soft yet firm kiss on my forehead, and then asked me to help with his packing.

I followed him to the bedroom, helping him as he prepared to leave in just an hour or two. After we finished packing, Dhruva went to the kitchen to make us some coffee. But then his phone vibrated. I walked over to check, and what I saw was disheartening. It was a text from Rashmika: *"Dhruva, I hope you're coming. I'm not well, and I need you."*

Confusion and anger bubbled inside me. Why did she need him? Why was my boyfriend the one she turned to? I placed the phone back and gathered my strength, preparing to confront Dhruva about the doubts gnawing at me.

When he returned with two mugs of coffee, he offered mine with a silent gesture, placing it on the side table. His eyes searched mine. "Is everything alright?" he asked, sensing my unease.

In a thin voice, I responded, "Yeah, all's well. Your phone was vibrating; I think you should check it." Then

I picked up my coffee and left the room, needing air to breathe.

He followed me, his face puzzled. "It was Vikrant, asking for my confirmation," he said.

His lie was blatant, his confidence in it unsettling. "Oh, so you saved his number with your ex's name, Rashmika? Strange."

His composure faltered. "You saw the text? Are you spying on me?"

"Dhruva? Do you still have the audacity to blame me here?" My voice wavered, my heart breaking. "I've ignored your social media posts, your stories with her, all those romantic pictures together even when you're supposed to be my boyfriend. I thought you loved me, that one day you'd realize my worth, but you've never forgotten her. I respected your feelings for her and never tried to ruin your friendship despite knowing your past. I believed you knew me better than anyone, that you loved me for who I am. Where are those feelings now?"

Tears streamed down my face as my heart shattered. "You betrayed me with your lies. You cheated on me for her. If you had just told me, I would have left without a word. But you chose to lie, to cheat. Why, Dhruva? What did I do wrong? Just because I refused to be in a physical relationship, you chose to leave me? Is that all that mattered?"

Dhruva broke his silence, his voice low. "You're wrong. I never loved you with those intentions. I liked you for who you are. I lied because I knew you were always jealous of Rashmika, and I didn't want to hurt you."

"Don't lie, Dhruva," I pleaded, my voice trembling. "Are you still dating her? Please, just tell me the truth."

"Yes," he admitted, his voice barely above a whisper. "I'm still dating her. I'm sorry, but I genuinely loved you. I wanted to keep our friendship intact, and I was afraid of losing you."

"You should have told me," I cried out, my pain palpable. "How could you do this to me?"

I ran to my room, tears blinding me, and locked the door. Dhruva knocked several times but eventually gave up, taking his bags and leaving the apartment without a goodbye.

I waited for him to break down the door, to shout at me, to stay and prove that this wasn't real, that he was still mine. But instead, he chose her over me again.

My tears, my heartache, were meaningless to him. Everything we shared, our laughs, our talks, our fights, our cuddles, kisses, hugs, our romance, even our families faded away in an instant.

If I could show him how much he meant to me, he would have regretted the day he chose to leave me. That day, I learned a harsh truth: no matter how deeply you love someone, they always have someone more important than you ever realized.

If you love too much, you're an emotional fool. If you don't believe in love, you're self-obsessed. If you lust after someone, you're branded a slut. And if you value emotions over physical intimacy, you're boring and naive.

"Souls can be crushed; memories are not always must but bodies over bodies are the only love, so we all should master the lesson of lust"

Two

Learning to Let Go

———

One year has passed, filled with memories of him and lingering dreams. I now work for an advertising agency in Delhi, residing in the same cosy and comfortable apartment where Dhruva and I once spent vacations together. His presence feels as vivid as ever, etched into my mind, while my heart clings to the hope that he might return to me.

In addition to my regular job, I've enrolled in a psychology class, which has been instrumental in my mental growth and healing. I've built a strong circle of friends, and my family, who live in our hometown of Indore, remains close despite the distance. It's a unique struggle to adapt to a new city, especially when it comes to cultural differences. The challenge, however, isn't just mine, it also lies in dealing with the judgmental and sometimes suffocating attitudes of those around us. I've always been able to brush off such negativity, remaining unfazed by those who accuse me of having a huge ego or forming other baseless opinions. I carry on, behaving as if I haven't noticed their remarks.

Everything seemed fine until one day when Ryan, a friend since my college days, shattered the peace. Ryan and I had shared countless conversations about business, spirituality, and comedy, despite our differences. We had always enjoyed each other's company, and even after college, we stayed in touch, joining the psychology class together. I never imagined that I would come to regret that decision.

After one class, we decided to grab coffee at a small café. The place was charming, with soft pink and white walls, unique hanging lamps, and white furniture that exuded comfort and calm. As we settled in, Reyan looked at me seriously and said, "Aadhvita, you're my best friend, but there's something I need to tell you. I don't like it when you post negative and emotional quotes online. Can you promise me you won't post anything like that for the next 25 days?"

I listened to him carefully, my reaction a mix of surprise and amusement. "Buddy, that's not possible," I replied. "It's my way of expressing myself, of lightening the weight on my heart."

Ryan seemed unfazed by my response. "I knew you'd say that," he said. "But if you don't agree, I'll stop talking to you forever."

His words hung in the air, and after a moment, I reluctantly agreed. We drank our coffee in silence, and as we walked home, we talked about mental health and its importance. Before parting ways, Reyan reminded me of my promise. I simply smirked in response, and we went our separate ways.

When I got home, the familiar ache of missing Dhruva hit me hard. His memories swirled around my mind, my body aching for his embrace, my lips craving his kiss. The harder I tried to escape these memories, the deeper I fell into them. My soul trembled with the onslaught of flashbacks. I dropped my bag on the sofa, changed, and began scrolling through Instagram while cooking rice to satisfy my hunger. That's when I saw a post of Dhruva with his new girlfriend. Their happy faces broke something inside me. In my pain, I posted a quote: "Dying is better than surviving in reality." That night, I fell asleep on the sofa, sobbing for the old, happy version of myself.

The next day, a harsh lesson awaited me, one I still struggle to understand. During the psychology class, I asked Ryan for his notes to fill in the points I'd missed, but he ignored me. I couldn't comprehend his sudden behaviour change. After class, when I tried to talk to him, he left with a new group, without a word to me.

A week passed with no interaction between us, and by then, I was too hurt to care. One evening, on my way home, I received an audio message from Ryan. My heart leapt with hope, thinking he finally wanted to talk. But as I played the message, my world crumbled. I collapsed on the road, tears streaming down my face. His words cut deeper than any wound: "You are the most selfish woman I've ever met. You use people, especially your so-called male friends, for your entertainment and then discard them when you're done, leaving them emotionally drained. Thank God I realised your true self early. Goodbye, Aadhvita. You'll never understand my worth. But why would you? You have a long line of guys waiting to give you a shoulder, right? Enjoy your life with those brats you deserve."

I felt utterly destroyed and emotionally shattered. It took me several minutes to gather the strength to move, to walk home as quickly as possible, desperate to reach a place where no one could see my pain. Even after I got home, I couldn't stop crying. I slammed the door shut and collapsed beside the sofa, hugging my bag tightly, and sobbing uncontrollably.

Suddenly, my phone rang. My fingers moved to answer it, despite my mind's resistance. I wasn't in the right state to talk, but my heart ached to hear the voice on the other end. Without thinking, I answered the call.

Three

Portraying New in 'Dark'

When his voice graced my ears, a soothing warmth washed over me, dissolving every ache. His mere sound stirred a deep longing within me, a yearning for his comforting embrace, where I could lay my heart bare, safe and enveloped in his presence. You might assume it was Dhruva calling, but no, it was Rudhvik, my friend since our school days. I tried to pull myself together, responding with a shaky voice, "Rudhvik, I wish you were here..." Then, I paused, the weight of my emotions threatening to break through.

"Adhvita? What's wrong? Why are you crying? Is everything alright? Where are you?" Rudhvik's voice, laced with panic, fired off questions in rapid succession. I could hear his breath quickening, betraying the urgency of his concern.

"Chill, Vik. I'm fine. Where are you? Finally, you found time to call after so long?" I tried to divert the conversation, masking my vulnerability.

But Vik, still tense, repeated his questions, his worry palpable. Then he finally answered, "I'm on my way to Indore from Bhopal."

"Why did you go to Bhopal?" I asked.

He hesitated, his voice low, "Official work."

"Okay," I replied, sensing something he wasn't saying.

"Aadhvita, please take care of yourself and don't cry. I hate it when you cry," he pleaded, his concern so genuine that it made my heart ache.

"I know," I whispered back, and he hung up. A small smile tugged at my lips as I stared at my phone screen, a mix of confusion and warmth swelling in my chest.

How could Vik, someone I've always seen as a reckless playboy whose life is a blur of drugs, and alcohol, but no romantic entanglements, be the one who so effortlessly calms my storm? I had never fully trusted him, wary of the way his eyes lingered on me and other girls, the way he seemed always on the verge of crossing a line that made me uneasy. Yet, despite my reservations, he held a special place in my life. He was my guide in moments of doubt, the one I confided in, drawn to his enigmatic personality despite my fears. He had proposed to me several times after school, but I had never seen him as more than a friend.

After what felt like an eternity, I finally mustered the strength to get up and prepare something to eat. Surprisingly, not a single thought about the Reyan incident crossed my mind. Instead, I felt an unfamiliar peace, a strange sense of strength, all thanks to Rudhvik. After dinner, which was pasta and coke I delved into my psychology studies, a wave of positivity washing over me. I checked my tasks from the office, sent out a few emails to clients, and then went to bed.

The next morning, around 9:00, the doorbell rang, startling me awake. I was confused, my heart pounding, as I wondered who could be at my door this early on a Saturday without informing me.

With hesitation and fear, I opened the door, and my breath caught in my throat. There, standing before me, was Rudhvik. Overwhelmed, I rushed to him, hugging him tightly as happy tears streamed down my cheeks. He wrapped his arms around me, lifting me off the ground and carrying me inside, closing the door behind him with one hand while the other held me close. We stayed like that for a moment, suspended in time, before he gently set me down. He then cupped my chin in his hand, tilting my face slightly to the left, and kissed my cheek with his soft, dark lips.

I looked up into his eyes, smiling with a joy I hadn't felt in ages. I took in his appearance, noticing how little had changed his wheatish complexion, sharper jawline, bushy eyelashes, and brows that I'd always admired. His smile, though rare, was as captivating as ever. He was the definition of handsome, his tall, fit body seemingly carved to perfection, capable of making any heart flutter.

"So, do you find me hotter this time?" he teased, his voice dripping with playful arrogance.

Clearing my throat, I replied, "Of course not. To me, you're still the same dumb, creepy guy you were in school, Vik."

He smirked, clearly amused. Still holding his luggage, a small trolley and a side bag slung over his shoulder he asked, "So, where can I put my stuff? Or is this how you welcome your guests?"

Feeling a bit embarrassed, I apologized and led him to the guest room, which was bigger than mine. The room's calming interior, a bed, a study table with a peaceful lamp, and a wardrobe was complemented by motivational quotes on the walls and a small bookshelf. The room's peaceful white colour scheme was broken only by a window near the entrance.

"This room doesn't suit my personality, Aadhvita. Don't you think?" he remarked, surveying the space.

"I know, Rudhvik. If you were staying longer, you could make changes, but you're not. So, let it be," I responded.

Rudhvik walked towards me as I stood by the door. He grabbed me, pulling me closer until my heartbeat quickened. He held my face with both hands, his thumbs gently caressing my cheeks as he tilted my face upwards to meet his gaze. His eyes shone with an intensity I couldn't decipher, his expression unreadable.

In a soft, seductive tone, he whispered, "I'll make this room mine if you want."

My mind went blank, my body frozen as I struggled to find words. "In your dreams," I finally managed to stammer.

He stepped even closer, his breath warm against my skin. I could feel the fire coursing through my veins, his lips grazing mine, teasing but not quite kissing. The sensation was overwhelming, and I couldn't bear it any longer. I shrugged him off, fleeing the room without looking back, and headed straight to the kitchen, my heart pounding and my body trembling.

Dhruva's name flashed in my mind. It was his touch, his presence that my body craved, the only thing that could match the intensity of what I had just felt with Rudhvik.

How could this be happening? My inner self battled with the thoughts of him, while my body still trembled from the moment that had left me shaken. I tried to calm my mind by distracting myself, heading to the kitchen to make us both a cup of coffee, hoping to forget the intensity of what had just transpired. Rudhvik remained in his room, but no matter how much I tried to push thoughts of him away, they kept resurfacing, stirring an unease I couldn't ignore.

With some effort, I managed to prepare the coffee and walked toward the sofa, placing one cup on the centre table before sitting down with mine. I took a sip, trying to focus on mundane tasks like grocery shopping, but my thoughts kept circling back to him.

Then, the door to his room creaked open, and he emerged, dressed in a black T-shirt and black jeans that made him look utterly ravishing. I bit my lower lip, determined not to let my gaze linger on him, and somehow, I managed to look away, trying to maintain some semblance of composure.

But he wouldn't allow that. Rudhvik came and sat next to me, his presence overwhelming. He held my chin with gentle yet firm hands, turning my face toward him, and forcing me to meet his gaze. "Ignoring me doesn't change what you felt in the guest room," he murmured, his voice soft but piercing. "I'm sorry for making you uncomfortable, especially around me."

His eyes were filled with an apology, their guilt and vulnerability cutting through my defences. I could feel myself weakening, both emotionally and physically, under the weight of his sincerity. Unable to speak, I leaned forward and kissed his forehead, my lips lingering against his skin for a moment before I pulled back with a soft smile. "It's okay," I whispered, meaning every word.

Rudhvik's eyes widened in surprise, and I could see the spark of joy that lit up his face, a joy so pure and unexpected that it warmed something deep within me. "Did you just kiss me?" he asked, his voice filled with wonder, and I nodded in affirmation, watching as his happiness overflowed, pulling me in even closer.

Overcome by a sudden, irresistible urge, I set my coffee mug back on the table and, without a second thought, I climbed onto his lap. His eyes widened further in surprise, "What are you up to?" he asked, his voice a mix of curiosity and anticipation.

I didn't reply. Instead, I cupped his face in my hands, feeling the warmth of his skin beneath my palms, and then, I closed the distance between us, pressing my lips to his in a tender and intense kiss. Time seemed to slow as I poured all my emotions into that kiss, feeling the way he responded with equal fervour, his arms wrapping around me, pulling me closer until there was no space left between us. The world outside faded, leaving only the two of us, lost in a moment that felt like it could last forever.

I opened my eyes to see him engrossed in the pleasure, both of his heads squeezing and massaging my thighs. I turned his face, biting his earlobes and saying, "How do you feel?" Then I began to softly kiss his cheek and turned to face him once more while grinning a little. His cheeks were blazing red, and I could see how happy he was as if it begged me to touch him again.

Has anyone ever appreciated my touch as much as he does now? How significant am I to him? If he can appreciate my touch

Then, to what extent will he cherish and love my sensations and emotions? I'm thinking about all of this till the silence breaks. What are you thinking?

I remained silent.

Has anyone ever commented on how adorable you are?

I reply with a giggle. Frequently

He gave me a sardonic look, raising his eyebrows, and said, "Of course, I asked, are you jealous?"

He uttered "Hmm!" Following a brief pause, he kissed my forehead and then moved to kiss the tip of my nose before moving to kiss my lips. He licked my lips, turning the kiss into a passionate smooch that made my veins tingle. I started to lose control. Before I know it, his cold, rough hands are pressing my bust, making me want more of him. My body is heating up, my hands are holding his hair, and my grip is getting tighter and tighter out of pleasure. He then throws me onto the sofa and moves over me without pausing the kiss he is lost in, gently kissing my chin before moving to my neck and sucking my skin. I sigh with pleasure as the fire in my body rises. I couldn't stop him then, as he crept down towards my bust and grinned while staring directly into my eyes. I want him to show me what it's like to experience physical closeness without having to tie each other down.

Despite the fact that I've always thought of Rudhvik as a playboy, his admiration for me has drawn me to him, and he asks for my trust so I can determine whether he genuinely loves me or just wants to use me like other people.

I'm not sure why, but my heart has always shown him to be a sincere person in my life who has never given up from the day we became friends. Even after eight years, he continues to be a strong emotional support system for me. However, one thing that makes me dislike him is his constant desire to touch me, which makes me uneasy and occasionally gives me an inappropriate vibe.

8 years back

It reminded me of my school days when Rudhvik and I were just good friends and he took me for a drive because he had brought a new bike that day. He then took me to his friend's house so we could sit and talk for a while, it was also a day I will never forget because he forced me to kiss him even though I wasn't ready and had refused. I will never forget that he kissed me against my will even though I was not ready for it and was refusing. His hold on my waist was so firm that I was unable to resist, and I screamed at him because I could not handle what had just happened my body had suddenly become weak and my entire dignity had been taken away from me in a fit of rage that made me start crying. What kind of upbringing have you received? and he moved away from me after that. The next event was spectacular. His facial expression was astonishing. His hands were shaking and his eyes were full of tears, but he controlled them from streaming down his cheeks. He bowed down in front of me and kept his head down, saying, "Sorry, my brain still can't process anything, and my body is still gathering strength, now what?" Rudhvik? This is why you took me here. He responded, to be honest, by staring up into my eyes while still kneeling and folding his legs, pleading for an apology. His eyes were blood red, and he said, in a shaky, indistinct voice, "No!" I never meant to do that, it just occurred that I repeatedly conveyed my affection for you. I genuinely adore you, Aadhvita. Is this how you feel about me? Rudhvik I sobbed uncontrollably on the ground, and Rudhvik quickly grabbed my face and felt my tears. I shoved him away in a rage, and he whispered, "I know I did wrong to you. I should have restrained myself so that I wouldn't have to do this with you. Let's head back home, where I'll speak with your parents and ask for your hand in marriage. Have you gone insane or what? in a bewildered and startled tone. His voice was confident, and tears were streaming down his cheeks. He apologised, held my hand to help me stand, and was about to leave his friend's room when I grabbed him and pulled him back, asking, "Are you serious?" His eyes met mine, and he confidently said, "Yes!" I swear that I will never again touch you without your permission because I love you, Aadhvita. Now, please allow me to speak to your parents about getting married. I said we were too young to get married, and then Rudhvik thought about what I had just said. I wiped my tears away, and he said, "I know I broke your trust, but I promise you that I will do anything to regain your trust and will marry you, I promise." I couldn't help but smile at his confidence, tears in my eyes.

Present time

When I see him now, his confidence remains unwavering. He shows me, through his actions, that he is truly there for me through all my ups and downs. Yes, he won my trust again, especially by standing by me during my most difficult moments. His promise to protect me and make me his is unshakable, yet the insecurities within me, the image of the "bad boy" he once was, linger like ghosts in the back of my mind. Despite his reassurances, my thoughts inevitably drift back to the past, to moments like the one when Rudhvik, lost in his world, gently caressed my lips with his thumb as he lay beside me on the sofa.

That memory was interrupted as Rudhvik whispered, "I love you, Aadhvita," pulling me closer to his chest. I locked eyes with him, my fingers gently holding his chin, and in a soft voice, I said, "I need time to figure out what is going on between us... and why. I don't find this appropriate..."

He immediately sat up, his face softening, but there was a sense of concern in his eyes. He helped me sit upright as well, and we both fell into a silence that stretched long and thick between us. I could feel the weight of the moment pressing on my chest, and though I wanted to speak, I just waited for him to say something.

Breaking the silence, he spoke first. "Say something, Vik... What? What is it, Aadhvita?" He turned to face me, his eyes searching mine for answers. "You think we're inappropriate? And your ex? You still need time?"

I hesitated, but he didn't give me the chance to explain. His disappointment was palpable, even before the words left his lips. "Okay, fine," he said, his voice barely above a whisper. Without another word, he stood up, and without even glancing back, he walked briskly towards the door. "Where are you going?" I called after him, my heart tightening.

"I'm going grocery shopping. I'll cook tonight," he replied curtly, his tone distant. He didn't look back as he slammed the door behind him, the sound of it reverberating in the room like a final nail in the coffin of our conversation. A heavy silence settled in my chest as I sank back onto the sofa, guilt gnawing at my insides. Had I hurt him this badly? My heart twisted with regret, but I couldn't deny that I needed time to understand myself, time to figure out where my feelings stood.

Hours passed. I buried myself in my work, revising notes from my last classes, though my mind kept drifting to Rudhvik. Each glance at my phone only added to the worry gnawing at me. Why hadn't I called him? What if I'd pushed him too far? It was already getting dark, and a knot of anxiety twisted tighter in my stomach. But I couldn't bring myself to reach out, fearing that my words might only make things worse. Just as I began to lose hope, the doorbell rang. I breathed out a sigh of relief, my heart leaping in my chest, hoping that Rudhvik had returned and that perhaps his mood had lightened.

I jumped up to answer the door, the weight on my chest easing slightly when I saw him standing there, bags of groceries in both hands. A smile tugged at my lips, and his expression softened, just a little. He raised an eyebrow, a playful gleam in his eye, as though his excitement about cooking was the thing that had pulled him out of the emotional fog. His cooking skills were unparalleled, and my mouth watered at the mere thought of the meal he was about to prepare. "What are you going to cook, Vik?" I asked, trying to bring a bit of normalcy back into the air between us. He smirked, his mood seeming to shift back into a lighter, more carefree version of himself. "You guess," he teased.

I watched as he kicked off his white Nike sneakers, the motion as casual as ever before he walked into the kitchen. The bags in his hands rustled as he placed them down on the counter, and with swift, practised movements, he began to unpack the ingredients. But then, he paused. For a moment, he stood still in the middle of the kitchen, scanning the space with a quiet intensity, as though trying to decide the next step or perhaps searching for something beyond the meal.

I stood quietly behind him, watching as he ran his fingers over the countertops, the subtle tension in his shoulders betraying the thoughts running through his mind. The familiar rhythm of his presence filled the space again, but there was something different in the air now, something unsaid between us that hung like a delicate thread waiting to snap. And yet, there was a kind of comfort in watching him. Even with the unspoken weight of our past and the uncertain future ahead of us, there was something undeniably reassuring in knowing he was here, cooking, offering a slice of normalcy when everything else felt like it was falling apart.

The kitchen interior that Vik tries to lose in to understand the surroundings is bathed in soft, natural light, with large windows that frame the view of the outside world. White walls, paired with warm wheatish cabinetry, create a sense of openness, while sleek, modern appliances subtly blend into the backdrop. The countertops are smooth, pale gray stone, reflecting a serene, understated elegance. A minimalist dining nook sits in one corner, with wooden chairs around a simple table. Above, gentle pendant lights cast a warm glow, enhancing the tranquil atmosphere. Each detail whether it's the clean lines of the shelves or the soft texture of woven baskets, invites calm and you to linger, as if time slows down within this peaceful, yet airy, space. The I interrupt him taking him back from his thoughts, where I you lost Vik he simply replied this apartment is made for you only calm and peaceful far from what my personality reflects I laughed at his silly yet sensible thought, you are not allowed to make changes here in the kitchen sorry with a kidding smile I teases him his smirk back at me with sarcasm you need any help Mr. Vik? he point me towards the eggs and asked me to boil it as he is cooking egg curry that he loved to eat so do I, but only when he or my mother cooks it.

Within no time the comforting aroma of spices slowly began to take over the room. Rudhvik was in his element, expertly stirring a pot of sizzling onions and tomatoes, his focus so intense it was almost endearing. I stood at the counter next to him, carefully placing eggs into a pot of water, her mind partially on the task but mostly on the warmth that filled my chest every time he smiled at me.

"You sure you're okay with the spices, the curry will be too hot," Rudhvik teased, glancing over at me as he added a pinch of garam masala. He is always kind, always full of unspoken things, flickered with mischief.

I rolled my eyes, but the hint of a smile tugged at the corners of my lips. "I said, though. "You just make things so... *extra spicy.*"

"Extra spicy? I was just helping you expand your palate," he shot back, his grin widening.

I laughed softly, reaching for the bowl of boiled eggs I'd already prepared. "If I expand my palate any more, I'll need a fire extinguisher in here."

He chuckled, a low sound that made my heart flutter, but I quickly pushed the feeling down. There had always been this easy rhythm between us, one that made everything feel comfortable, light. I told myself that was all it was. We are best friends. Nothing more.

But as I cracked the shells off the eggs, I couldn't ignore the fluttering that always seemed to start up in my chest whenever he was near. Or when he laughed. Or when our fingers brushed accidentally as we reached for the same spoon. These little things, these seemingly insignificant moments, made me question the boundaries of our friendship.

Rudhvik was humming a tune under his breath, focused on frying onions in the pan, oblivious to the war raging quietly inside of me. I handed him the bowl of eggs without looking up, hoping he wouldn't notice the slight tension in my shoulders.

"You're doing it again," Rudhvik said suddenly, his voice serious now, and it snapped her back to reality.

"Doing what?" I asked, my voice a bit sharper than I intended, but I couldn't help it. I felt exposed somehow.

He paused for a moment, setting down the spatula, and turned to face her fully. There was a warmth in his gaze, the kind that made my stomach twist. "You're thinking about something," he said softly. "You've been distant all day."

I shifted uncomfortably, biting my lip. It wasn't like I could lie to him, not after all these years. He knew her too well.

"I'm fine," I said, though the words felt hollow even as I said them. I could feel the heat of his gaze on me, searching, knowing that something wasn't right.

Rudhvik took a step closer, his presence calm and steady, as always. "You know you can talk to me about anything, right?" he asked, his voice so gentle it made my heart ache.

I nodded, trying to smile, but my lips trembled slightly. "I know. It's just..." I trailed off, unable to put my feelings into words.

He studied her for a long moment, as if trying to figure out what she wasn't saying. And then, with a quiet understanding, he reached for a couple of eggs and cracked them into the pan, the sizzling sound filling the quiet space between them.

"Well, I'm still going to make this curry extra spicy," he said lightly, nudging her with his elbow.

I couldn't help but laugh, the tension melting away for a brief moment. The kitchen was filled with the familiar warmth of their inside jokes and shared comfort. It was moments like this moments of laughter and easy closeness that reminded her how much he meant to me maybe. But as much as my heart yearned to acknowledge the feelings that I'm still not able to figure out and don't intend to understand at this moment, I wasn't ready to let them surface.

Not yet.

Rudhvik didn't push,

We continued cooking together, laughing and joking and simply existing in the space we had always shared. But somewhere, in the quietest corners of my heart, For now, I was content to be with him, just as we were cooking, laughing, and, for a moment, feeling like everything was right in the world.

After an hour of hard work, we finally sat at the dining talve together and ready to have the food then suddenly Rudhvik surprised me with a wine's the party began I was so happy and excited

The night had drifted into a hazy blur, with the flickering light making it look a little dark, perfect for a dinner on the dining table where Rudhvik and I sat. The dim glow of the room mimicked the warmth that had settled between us, a familiar, comfortable silence that spoke volumes. We'd just finished dinner, and the last of the wine had been poured into our glasses. The taste of rich red wine lingered on my tongue as I took another sip, feeling the alcohol starting to seep into my system, loosening the tightness in my chest, but also dulling my senses a bit.

Rudhvik was quiet for a moment, looking at me across the table with an intensity that made my heart race. His eyes were steady, unwavering, and there was something about the way he looked at me tonight that felt different. His gaze was softer, more tender as if he was holding something back, something important.

I wiped the back of my hand across my lips, feeling the warmth of the wine flush through my cheeks. My mind felt foggy, but I couldn't stop myself from speaking. Maybe it was the alcohol loosening my inhibitions, or perhaps it was just the weight of everything I had been suppressing for so long.

"You know, Rudhvik," I started, my voice low, almost too soft, but the words were already spilling out. "I... I think I'm starting to understand something. Something about you. About... us."

He raised an eyebrow, his fingers slowly tapping against the glass in front of him, but his expression showed no hint of surprise. He was used to me being unpredictable, but tonight, something in my tone made him pause.

"Yeah?" he asked quietly, a little smile tugging at the corner of his lips. "What are you understanding?"

I took another drink, feeling the warmth spread through my chest, but I knew the truth was spilling out, whether I wanted it to or not.

"I'm afraid of you," I blurted out, the words hanging heavy in the air. "I know that sounds crazy, but it's the truth. You… you're not like everyone else. You *were* a bad boy, and I can't seem to shake that image of you, even now. And then there was that… incident with the kiss."

I could see the flicker of hurt in his eyes, but he didn't interrupt. He didn't move, didn't say anything. He simply let me speak, the same as he always did. His patience, that unshakable, calming presence, made me want to spill everything.

"But the thing is, Rudhvik," I continued, my words a little slurred, "You've been there for me. For so many years. You've been… you've always been there. You've never let me go, even when I pushed you away. And I can't help but feel like… maybe, just maybe, you're not what I thought you were. You're not the guy I thought you were."

I looked at him, my eyes clouded with the vulnerability I hadn't let anyone see in years. The words hung between us like fragile threads, waiting to be severed.

Rudhvik didn't say anything for a long moment, but when he finally spoke, his voice was thick with emotion.

"I'm not perfect, Aadhvita. I never was. But I love you. I've always loved you. In ways you'll never understand." His gaze was unwavering, his confidence radiating, as if he had waited years to say this.

My heart skipped a beat, but then a wave of doubt and confusion washed over me. I wasn't ready to hear it. Not like this, not now. My head was still tangled in memories of Dhruva of the pain, the betrayal, the confusion.

"Rudhvik," I murmured, my voice barely above a whisper. "I don't know if I can—"

"Hey," he cut in softly, moving around the table to sit next to me. "You don't have to say anything right now. I know it's complicated. Just... just know that I'm here. I'll wait for you. Always."

I nodded, but there was a heaviness in my chest that I couldn't shake. The alcohol had made me speak the truth, but it hadn't made it any easier to accept.

Before I knew it, he was helping me stand, his arm steady around my waist as he guided me toward my bedroom. The room spun slightly, and I clung to him for balance, trying to ignore the rush of feelings crashing into me like waves against the shore.

Once inside, he closed the door softly behind us, and I leaned against the bed, trying to steady myself.

"You're drunk," Rudhvik murmured, but there was no judgment in his voice, just an understanding that made my heart ache. "I'm not going anywhere, okay? Just... relax."

His hands were gentle as he helped me out of my clothes, the familiar touch making my heart pound in a way I wasn't prepared for. I wanted to tell him to stop, to tell him that I wasn't ready, but his presence was so calming, so reassuring, that the words got caught in my throat. He moved slowly, his hands lingering on my skin, as if he was giving me time to pull away if I wanted to.

But I didn't pull away. I let him help me change into something more comfortable, the soft fabric of my pajamas making me feel safe in his hands.

Then, without saying anything more, Rudhvik climbed into the bed beside me. He pulled me into his arms, his warmth enveloping me like a shield, and I could feel the steady beat of his heart against mine. His hands gently caressed my back, and the slow, rhythmic motion lulled me into a peaceful state of surrender.

"You're safe here, Aadhvita," he whispered in his voice like a balm for my wounded heart. "You don't have to rush. We'll take this one step at a time, okay?"

I closed my eyes, the weight of the world slowly melting away. His tenderness, his honesty, his love was all so overwhelming, and yet, for the first time in so long, I felt like I could breathe again.

And then, the most unexpected thing happened: I fell asleep, right there in his arms. The steady rise and fall of his chest was a lullaby that pulled me deeper into sleep, into a place where my past didn't haunt me, where I could simply feel.

Rudhvik, ever the protector, stayed awake just a little longer, his fingers gently stroking my hair. His heart, just as steady and strong as always, kept beating in rhythm with mine. It wasn't intimacy. Not in the way I was used to understanding it. But it was something deeper, something more real than I'd ever known.

And as I drifted into slumber, I knew one thing for sure: I was no longer just afraid of him. The boy who once seemed like trouble was now the man I trusted more than anyone in this world.

The morning could wait. Tonight, I was safe, wrapped in his arms, and for the first time in a long time, I was at peace.

Four

New Blue Without Clues

———•———

The morning light filtered softly through the curtains, gently waking me up. As I opened my eyes, I found myself lying next to Rudhvik, his peaceful face soft in slumber, his chest rising and falling in a rhythm that calmed me. For a moment, a blur of memories rushed through my mind flashbacks of last night. I remembered how he had carefully helped me change my clothes when I was drunk, his touch both tender and steady, guiding me as if I were fragile. His care and attention had been both awkwardly endearing and comforting, leaving me with a strange mix of feelings: shy, yet safe and secure. His presence had washed over me in a way that made me feel protected, even though I hadn't fully processed the depth of it all.

I quietly slipped out of bed, careful not to disturb him, and padded across the room to

take a quick bath. Afterward, I threw my damp hair into a messy ponytail and slipped into a comfortable oversized neon pink t-shirt and a pair of blue denim shorts. The loose, casual look gave me a carefree, cute vibe sexy in its simplicity, yet comforting in its own way.

I made myself a cup of coffee and took a seat at the dining table, where my laptop was waiting. I began sifting through emails, feeling the weight of my workday settling over me. With each message I read, the minutes passed slowly. Two hours later, it was 9:00 am, and the sun had risen sharply, casting a brilliant glow across the sky. I stared out the window, seeking a moment of clarity, of refreshment from the new day. But just as I lost myself in the view, I saw Rudhvik, standing in the doorway, staring at me. His loose grey pajama bottoms and oversized white t-shirt made him look effortlessly strong, his muscles evident beneath the fabric. I couldn't help but steal a quick glance, though I quickly looked away, embarrassed by my own attraction.

"Good morning," I said, smiling widely, feeling the freshness of the new day surge through me.

He sat down next to me, his brow furrowing slightly as he glanced at the screen. "Aren't you going to the office?"

I froze, unsure of how to respond. I didn't want to face the world today, not after everything. But I couldn't bring myself to tell him why. I had a long history of keeping my vulnerabilities tucked away, especially with him. "Kind of," I muttered, "I don't really want to face people right now."

I felt the heaviness of my words weigh on the air, but I couldn't bring myself to elaborate. "I felt humiliated," I continued, though it wasn't even enough to begin explaining the emotional drain I felt after the Ryan incident. I didn't want to tell Rudhvik how emotionally exhausted I was, how the world felt like too much. I couldn't bear to see the anger in his eyes if I told him about Ryan. He'd probably lash out, and I didn't want to deal with that.

Rudhvik's face shifted, the concern in his eyes deepening. "Tell me what's wrong?"

I couldn't bring myself to explain. I stood up quickly, retreating to the kitchen to make myself another cup of coffee, trying to avoid his gaze, trying to shake off the emotions that were threatening to overwhelm me.

But before I could retreat too far, I felt his hand on my arm. He gently pulled me back toward him. "Sit down," he requested softly, but with an underlying force. "You're not getting away this time. You're going to tell me the truth."

I couldn't hide anymore. I had to tell him, or I'd break under the weight of it. With a shaky breath, I sat back down, the warmth of the coffee in my hands offering me a small semblance of comfort. I finally let it all out the pain I'd been holding in for the past week, the humiliation, the raw vulnerability that I'd never fully allowed myself to feel. I told Rudhvik everything, the shame, the pain, the crushing sense of abandonment. When I finished speaking, my tears were still flowing, uncontrollably. But he didn't say anything at first. Instead, he pulled me into his arms, holding me tightly as if he could shield me from the world's cruelty.

And even though I couldn't stop crying, there was something about his embrace, the way he held me close, that made everything feel just a little bit bearable. I felt his anger quiet, simmering beneath the surface but he didn't say a word. He didn't need to. His protective Aadhvitaure was already speaking louder than anything else.

For the first time in days, I felt a small flicker of hope. Maybe I wasn't as alone in this as I thought.

The air between Rudhvik and me crackled with tension, an unspoken storm ready to break. His voice, raw and seething with anger, shattered the fragile silence that had descended between us. "Get ready. I'm taking you to your classes," he commanded. There was a fury in his words, a protective rage that I knew well. It was not the kind of anger that sought to control, but the kind that sought to shield, to defend what was precious to him. And yet, the very strength of his command sent a shiver of fear through me, not because I feared him, but because I feared how Rudhvik would react if saw Ryan

Ryan's words echoed in my mind, cutting through my thoughts like a blade as if they had been carved into the very marrow of my being. "You didn't listen to me," he had said, his voice cold and filled with venom. "You couldn't even do the one thing I asked you to post for twenty-five days, just a simple act of positivity, and you forgot. You ruined everything." The accusation had struck me like a lightning bolt, too swift and too sharp for me to grasp hold of any semblance of defense. The words hung in the air, a suffocating weight, pressing down on me, suffocating the last shreds of my self-worth.

I had forgotten. I hadn't meant to ignore him. I hadn't meant to hurt him. But in my mind, amidst the chaos of everything else, I had allowed the world to slip through my fingers. A simple request, one that seemed so trivial in the grand scheme of my life, had become a mountain I couldn't scale. And Ryan, in his hurt and frustration, had turned against me, as though I were an enemy, an adversary to be castigated. His words, filled with disdain, cut through me. They carved into my spirit, branding me with the name of failure.

His hatred was not just a product of my forgetfulness; it was a reflection of how little he thought of me. In his eyes, I had betrayed him. I had betrayed the trust he had placed in me, and that betrayal had made me worthless, invisible, as if the friendship we had shared meant nothing. To him, I was an afterthought, a careless friend who could not fulfill even the simplest of promises. The harshness in his tone made me feel small, insignificant, and utterly alone. In his eyes, I had become something less than human, nothing more than a disappointment, a broken promise.

As Rudhvik's voice broke through my thoughts, the weight of his words felt like an anchor pulling me deeper into the abyss. "Get ready," he repeated, his anger now tinged with concern. His love for me was evident, as much as it frightened me. I knew how deeply he cared, how fiercely he would protect me. But the thought of facing Ryan's wrath, of hearing the same harsh words echoed back to me, made my insides tremble with dread.

I didn't want to go. I couldn't face the world. I couldn't face the people who looked at me as if I were no more than a shell of the person I had once been. So much had changed, and with it, my sense of self had been chipped away, piece by piece, until there was little left but a shadow, an empty vessel, filled with nothing but the remnants of the person I used to be.

In that moment, I felt the weight of the world pressing down on me, squeezing the breath from my lungs. My body felt heavy, as though the very air around me was too thick to move through. I couldn't stand it. I couldn't run. I could barely lift my hand to reach for Rudhvik's, but somehow, I found the strength to grasp it. His warmth, his steady presence, was the only thing that grounded me in that moment.

"Vik," I whispered, my voice breaking on the fragile breath I took. "I don't want to go."

Tears welled up in my eyes, though they seemed too exhausted to fall anymore. I had cried until I thought there were no more tears left in me, but the wound Ryan had inflicted was too deep. The shame, the guilt, the sense of worthlessness had become an unbearable weight. I could feel it sinking into my skin, into my bones, spreading through me like poison. And as much as Rudhvik's presence was a balm, it could not erase the scar Ryan had left.

He sat beside me, his hand gently enveloping mine, offering solace. But even his comfort felt fleeting. I was not sure how he would react. He, too, was hurt by Ryan's treatment of me. I could see it in the way his eyes darkened with pain when he spoke of him. Would he, too, turn his anger upon me? Would he blame me for everything that had happened, for allowing Ryan's harsh words to wound me so deeply? The fear that he might see me as weak, as undeserving of his protection, gnawed at me. I feared that he might believe Ryan's version of the truth that I had somehow ruined everything. That I had failed.

But worse still was the truth that I had already failed myself. I had allowed Ryan to see me as something worthless, something unworthy of care. His words had seeped into the very fabric of my soul, leaving me broken, hollow. I couldn't shake the feeling that I would never be whole again, that the scars he had left would never fade. As a woman, I felt the sharp sting of judgment, of being seen as something fragile, something incapable of fulfilling even the smallest of expectations. Ryan's betrayal had cut me deeper than any of his words could explain, because it wasn't just his words that hurt—it was the realization that I had let myself become someone who was incapable of standing up for herself.

I lowered my head, unable to face the world, unable to face the future that seemed so uncertain, so alien. "Vik," I whispered again, "I don't know how to face them. I don't know how to face anyone anymore."

The world outside the walls of our home seemed so vast, so cruel. The thought of stepping into it, of confronting the weight of my failures and my fears, seemed unbearable. My body ached with the exhaustion of holding it all in of trying to appear strong when inside, I was crumbling. The scar Ryan had left on me was not just a physical mark. It was a wound to my spirit, one that had drained me of my confidence, my strength. And though Rudhvik was beside me, offering his quiet comfort, I knew that I was the only one who could begin to heal. But I didn't know how.

The morning air felt too heavy as I stood beside Rudhvik, my mind a whirlwind of emotions. I hadn't realized how deeply Ryan's words had cut until now, until Rudhvik's presence seemed to awaken something inside me, something I had buried long ago. His voice, calm and steady, broke through the chaos inside me as he spoke with such unwavering certainty.

"Aadhvita," he said, his voice wrapping around me like a protective shield, "you are a strong woman. You can rule the world with your pure intentions and your simple, unpretentious way of being. You heal everyone around you with your positivity and your light. You can't give up now. Trust me, I'm with you, and I'll never let anyone hurt you again. Not as long as I'm here."

I felt my heart tighten, my chest swell with emotions I couldn't fully name. There was something about the way he said it, the sincerity in his eyes, that made it feel like the world could be a little less harsh. I had never heard such conviction in someone's words before. He pulled the chair closer to him, his presence overwhelming and comforting at the same time. Then, in a soft, intimate gesture, he held my chin gently and kissed my forehead, a kiss that spoke volumes without uttering a single word.

"You don't need to justify yourself, Aadhvita. I know who you are, and so do the people who matter. They believe in you and love you exactly the way you are the strongest, the loudest, the most vibrant character. You are a queen, Aadhvita. A queen who roars with positivity and purity. That's who you are, my girl."

I couldn't believe it. It was Rudhvik, the one person who saw me not for my flaws but for the strength in my soul. The weight in my chest, the bitterness in my heart from Ryan's cruel words, began to lift, just a little. His words built a bridge over the chasm of self-doubt that had grown too wide. A smile, small but genuine, broke across my face, and a soft chuckle escaped my lips.

"Really?" I whispered, my voice thick with the emotion I was struggling to hold back. "Thank you... so much." I could feel the walls I had built around myself slowly crumbling as his warmth and faith seeped in. For the first time in what felt like forever, I felt seen, truly seen, and accepted.

With his words, my insecurities, my fears, and the weight of Ryan's judgment seemed to evaporate into the air. I felt strong again, no longer just a woman haunted by past hurts, but someone with the power to shape her future. Looking up into his eyes, I felt something shift within me, something I had never allowed myself to acknowledge before. "I... I think I'm falling for you," I murmured, almost too shy to admit it, but it felt right.

A playful smile tugged at Rudhvik's lips, his eyes glinting with amusement. "I wish," he teased softly, and that smile of his sent a flutter straight to my heart.

I stood, shaking off the moment's weight as I prepared to get ready. Comfort was my first priority, and today, more than ever, I needed to feel grounded. My fingers worked through my hair, gathering it into a high ponytail, and I slipped into my oversized neon pink T-shirt and blue denim shorts. I threw on my white sneakers and made my way out of the room, calling for Rudhvik.

"Let's go, Vik."

He appeared a moment later, dressed as he always was effortlessly cool in his black jeans, oversized black T-shirt, and black boots. The man seemed to radiate a quiet confidence that made my heart beat a little faster. Without wasting any time, we left the apartment and jumped into a cab, heading toward my psychology classes.

The morning sun cast a gentle warmth through the cab window, but inside, a storm was brewing. When we arrived at the institute, I could feel the tension crawling up my spine. As we entered the reception area, my heart pounded in my chest. I wasn't sure I was ready for what lay ahead, but Rudhvik's presence by my side kept me grounded.

Mrs. Shikha, my counselor, greeted us with a warm smile. She was an older woman, probably in her mid-40s, dressed in a yellow coordiAadhvitaed set that gave her an air of authority. She had an undeniable confidence, and though her age made her appear overworked, her sharp gaze missed nothing. She asked about my well-being and immediately shifted her focus to Rudhvik, curious about who he was.

Rudhvik, ever calm and composed, introduced himself, and she invited us to her office. The room was pristine, with white walls that gave it a sterile, clinical feel. The motivational quotes hanging on the walls reflected the environment—suitable for someone in her profession, but nothing that could soothe the rawness in my chest. We sat down, and as Rudhvik began to recount the events with Ryan, he squeezed my hand gently, a silent reassurance that he was right there with me, no matter what.

Mrs. Shikha's expression shifted from surprise to sadness as she processed the information. She then asked me to go into my mentor's office to write an application against Ryan, so the institute could take appropriate action.

As her words hung in the air, I looked up at Rudhvik, seeking his opinion. He nodded, his gaze unwavering. "I'm here with you, Aadhvita. If you feel uncomfortable at any moment, just scream my name. I'll run to you."

I nodded reluctantly, feeling the weight of the decision pressing down on me. But before I could move, I noticed something at a glance from Mrs. Shikha, not at me, but at Rudhvik. She stared at him for an uncomfortably long time, not even blinking. I felt a cold wave of disgust rise in me and cleared my throat loudly, hoping to snap her out of whatever foolish trance she was in.

When I finally made my way to the mentor's office, it was no surprise that Ms. Sidra was there, her presence too smug and self-assured for my taste. She was fair-skinned, with long hair that framed her face like a picture, but to me, she had always come across as arrogant and condescending. I didn't like her at all.

She offered me a seat, and as I sat across from her, she immediately apologized for what had happened. She handed me a blank sheet of paper, a pen, and asked me to write the application. But as I glanced toward the classroom next door, I noticed the glass walls that separated us from the rest of the institute. Ryan's absence gave me some comfort, but I still felt exposed. I refused to write the application.

"I don't want to ruin Ryan's career," I said, my voice shaking slightly. "I don't want to be the one responsible for it."

Ms. Sidra, however, assured me that nothing would happen to him. "It's just a warning, Aadhvita. Nothing more," she said, her tone dismissive, like she was above any real concern for me.

Eventually, I gave in, the weight of the decision pulling me into compliance. I submitted the application, and as I was about to leave, Ms. Sidra stopped me with a request to sit down once more.

She scanned me from head to toe, her gaze lingering far too long. I felt a rush of discomfort, like every inch of my skin was suddenly exposed, under her judgmental eye. Then, her words pierced me like shards of glass.

"Did you come here to showcase your body, Aadhvita? Is this how you intend to get the attention of the boys here? Wearing shorts and exposing your legs is not appropriate. If you're going to be in this institution, you need to cover up. Show some respect."

The disgust rose so quickly in me that I thought I might choke on it. My fists clenched at my sides, my heart racing with a fury I hadn't known I was capable of. How dare she? How dare she reduce me to my clothing, to my body?

I stood up so quickly that my chair nearly toppled. "Ms. Sidra, I think you need to cleanse your mind before you dare to speak to me like that!" My voice rang out, full of fury, as I slammed my fist onto her desk. "Your dirty thinking isn't my problem. And don't ever disrespect me again."

With that, I stormed out of her office, leaving her dumbstruck and stammering behind me. The glass walls in the hallway seemed to blur as I walked past, my anger turning into something cold and bitter, something that would stay with me for a long time.

I rushed down to the parking lot, where the cab was waiting for me. My heart was still racing, my hands shaking.

I needed to get out of here. As I waited for Rudhvik, who was still inside, I made a decision. I was done. I was done with this institution, done with the humiliation, the disrespect, and the toxic environment. This place had only brought me scars, and I refused to stay any longer.

I was stronger than this. I had to be.

As the clock ticked away, my body was still shaking from the whirlwind of emotions that had engulfed me in the past few hours. The anger, the humiliation, and the relief of finally taking a stand were all crashing over me in waves. I couldn't stop my hands from trembling as I waited outside the institution, my breath shallow, my mind racing. I was done. I had made up my mind to quit this place, but the weight of that decision still pressed down on my chest.

Then, suddenly, a familiar figure appeared. Through the parking lot, I saw Rudhvik, his face creased with worry as he sprinted toward me. The sight of him brought a sense of calm to the chaos within me, but his urgency the way he rushed toward me without a second thought sent a shiver of warmth through my veins.

Without a word, he reached me and took my hand. His touch, steady and strong, seemed to anchor me in the storm of emotions that had been swirling around me all day. I glanced up at him, but his gaze was focused, his brow furrowed with concern.

"I'm sorry," he said, his voice soft but sincere, the words a balm for the rawness I hadn't even realized I was carrying. "I should've paid more attention when you asked me to come with you. I should've been there."

I shook my head, trying to brush off his apology, not wanting to add more weight to what was already a heavy day. "It's okay," I murmured, my voice barely audible as I fought to steady myself. "It's just... I've decided to quit. I'm done with this institution. I can't be here anymore."

The words left my mouth like a weight lifting from my shoulders. Saying it out loud made it feel like I had taken control of the situation, like I had reclaimed my power. But there was still an undercurrent of fear, of uncertainty, that I couldn't quite shake.

Rudhvik's eyes softened, and he nodded, as if he understood completely. His hand tightened around mine, and he asked quietly, "What happened, Aadhvita? What made you decide this?"

I took a deep breath, trying to steady my trembling hands. I could feel the heat rise in my chest as I thought about Ms. Sidra's words. The anger, still raw and bitter, surged through me.

"She... she commented on my clothes, Rudhvik. She disrespected me in a way that I can't ignore. She told me that wearing shorts like this was inappropriate, that I was 'showing off my body' to get attention. And it just... it hurts, you know? To be reduced to nothing more than the clothes I wear."

As I spoke, the anger bubbled to the surface again, and I felt a knot tighten in my stomach. But before I could get lost in the bitterness, Rudhvik's hand gently rubbed the palm of mine, a silent comfort that grounded me once more. His touch was steady, firm, and it calmed the storm inside me.

"I'm so sorry, Aadhvita," he whispered, his eyes dark with sympathy. "No one has the right to make you feel like that. Especially not someone like her."

We didn't need to say anything more. His words were a balm, and for the first time all day, I felt like I could breathe a little easier. The anger started to recede, and in its place, there was a quiet understanding between us. He was here for me, and that was all I needed to know.

We reached home a little while later, both of us too drained to do anything but change into more comfortable clothes. The pizza we ordered was a welcome distraction, its warm, cheesy goodness filling the air with a sense of normalcy after the chaos of the day. By the time we finished eating, it was around 7 PM, and the kitchen was clean, but my mind was still buzzing.

I felt the exhaustion from the emotional rollercoaster of the day settling in, and I didn't even try to fight it. I headed straight to my room, feeling my body collapse onto the bed with a soft sigh. I closed my eyes, but just as I was about to drift off, I heard footsteps behind me. I opened my eyes to see Rudhvik standing in the doorway, his expression playful but with a hint of something deeper, something I couldn't quite place.

"What?" I asked, confusion flickering in my voice as I met his gaze.

His eyes sparkled with a mischievous glint, and a smirk spread across his face. Without a word, he extended his hand toward me. The playful energy in his gaze made my heart skip a beat. What was he up to?

Then, with a flourish, he pulled out his phone, flicked on the flashlight, and pressed play on a song. The familiar chords of Tequila by Dan + Shay filled the room, and for a moment, everything else faded away. The weight of the day, the stress, the humiliation, the exhaustion seemed to disappear as I looked at him. He was already grinning, his eyes filled with a joy that was infectious.

I hesitated at first, feeling a little self-conscious after everything that had happened, but the joy in his eyes was too much to resist. He made me feel seen, valued, and loved in a way no one else had before. And in that moment, I realized that I didn't need to worry about the opinions of others. Not when I had someone who saw me for who I really was.

I stood, taking his hand with a soft smile, and let the music take over. We began to dance, our movements at first tentative, unsure, but slowly becoming more confident as we laughed at our own awkwardness. I wasn't concerned about being graceful or perfect, I was just... happy.

For the next two hours, time seemed to blur. Every silly dance move, every burst of laughter, every moment of shared joy added another layer to the bond between us. We moved together, our feet shuffling and spinning, sometimes stumbling, but always laughing, always finding joy in the ridiculousness of it all. Rudhvik's laughter was infectious, and soon, I found myself dancing like no one was watching, not caring about the world outside the walls of this room.

The time slipped away faster than I could have imagined, and soon enough, our feet began to ache, the exhaustion catching up with us. We collapsed onto the bed, side by side, our bodies sore from the spontaneous dancing but our hearts light with the kind of joy that only comes when you are fully present in the moment. I could feel Rudhvik's warmth beside me, his breath steady as we both drifted into a peaceful sleep.

In that quiet moment, as I closed my eyes and let the rhythmic sound of his breathing soothe me, I felt something shift inside. The worries, the fears, and the insecurities that had once clouded my mind seemed to melt away, leaving only the certainty that, no matter what happened next, I had someone who believed in me. Someone who made me feel strong when the world tried to make me small.

And in that deep, peaceful sleep, for the first time in a long time, I felt truly at peace.

Five

Letting the Wings Shed Away

———•◆•———

The days that followed began to blend together in a rhythm I wasn't used to, but it felt oddly comforting. It had been a month since Rudhvik and I had started living together, and, despite the minor bumps along the way, life was settling into a new, unexpected normal. Rudhvik had adjusted to his new role as a web developer, and with it came a sense of purpose that he carried with grace. It was as though the weight of his responsibilities helped him grow even more into the man I was coming to admire and respect.

He had made quite a few changes to the apartment most notably, the guest room, which, as expected, was no longer a guest room. In fact, it felt more like his domain now. What was once a simple, neutral space had been transformed into his sanctuary: a mini gym with a grey and white theme. The room felt cool, calm, and meticulously ordered, like a place where both his body and mind could find solace. A few paintings of leaves and birds adorned the walls, his subtle way of bringing the outdoors inside, a reflection of his quiet and introspective nature.

The one thing I genuinely appreciated in his room was the bookshelf, a small but meaningful collection of books about Indian history, something that spoke to his deep-rooted love for knowledge. I often found myself lost in its pages, drawn to the way history unfolded in those books, just as I was getting lost in the quiet ways Rudhvik made me feel safe, valued, and loved. And those quiet moments of respect and understanding between us were slowly chipping away at the walls I had built around myself.

I couldn't quite put my finger on it, but with each passing day, I smiled more. My laughter came more easily. The memories of Dhruva, once so painfully close to my heart, no longer had the same grip on me. The sharp pangs of sorrow still came, yes, but they were fewer now. And it wasn't that I had forgotten Dhruva, but rather, I had learned to make peace with it. Rudhvik's constant support, his quiet ways of showing affection, had softened the rough edges of my heart.

But my feelings for him remained unclear. Sometimes I felt the stirrings of something more something deeper but it was always shadowed by the fear of vulnerability, the fear of opening myself up entirely again. The respect I had for him was undeniable, but something more complex lingered in the corners of my heart. It was a tug-of-war I wasn't entirely sure I was ready to face.

One evening, the shift between the uncertainty and the affection became painfully apparent. I had just finished a long day at work and was about to relax when, unexpectedly, my period hit. The cramps were sharp and unrelenting, seizing my body and leaving me paralyzed in bed. I could barely move as the pain gnawed at my insides, turning my legs into heavy weights, numb with discomfort.

It wasn't the first time I'd experienced this, but it was the worst in recent memory. The only thing I managed to do was open the door when I heard Rudhvik's footsteps approach. He walked in, already holding his keys in his hand, but when his eyes fell on me, his expression shifted immediately.

"What happened?" he asked, concern thick in his voice as he dropped his bag by the door.

I looked up at him, feeling a wave of embarrassment rise in my chest. My face flushed with a mix of shyness and discomfort. "I'm on my periods... the pain's just... unbearable."

Without another word, Rudhvik did something that caught me completely off guard. His brow furrowed, his concern deepening, and before I could protest, he dropped his bag to the floor and swooped me up into his arms.

I gasped in surprise, my heart racing as he gently lifted me and carried me to the bed, laying me down with a tenderness I had never experienced from anyone before. His hands were gentle, as though I were fragile, but his presence, his strength was unwavering.

"You should've told me sooner," he murmured, his voice filled with genuine worry. It was the kind of worry I had only ever seen from family, but there was something more in his eyes. Something that made me feel safe.

I tried to reassure him, though I could tell he wasn't convinced. "It's okay... I'm used to it," I said softly, though the pain still lingered.

"I don't care if you're used to it, Aadhvita," he replied, his voice firm but caring. "You shouldn't have to go through this alone."

Rudhvik insisted I rest, so I settled back into the covers while he left to freshen up. The tenderness of his actions and the quiet care he gave me felt foreign, yet deeply comforting. I wanted to protest, to tell him I was fine, but something in me, some deeper, unspoken part recognized the rarity of this kind of affection.

When he returned, I had drifted off to sleep, my body exhausted from the pain. But I woke to find him sitting next to me, gently caressing my hair and brushing his fingers over my forehead. His touch was soothing, almost healing in its simplicity. He was there, present, in a way that made the world outside seem insignificant.

"Wake up, Aadhvita," he whispered. "Look, I made you your favorite pasta."

I blinked, my senses still heavy with sleep, and turned to see a plate of pasta sitting on the bedside table. He had cooked it himself. The realization hit me like a wave, and for the first time in days, I felt a warmth spread through me. Rudhvik had taken the time to care for me not out of obligation, but because he wanted to.

As I sat up, he fed me the pasta with his own hands, a small but profound act of affection. There were chocolates, too, and ice cream, all the things I hadn't even asked for, yet somehow, he knew exactly what I needed.

After I had eaten, he insisted we take a walk in the garden. I was reluctant, not wanting to get dirty or move too much, but he wouldn't let me refuse. His gentle insistence was a reminder of the safety he gave me, a safety I had longed for but never quite believed could exist outside of family. We walked slowly, side by side, him always by my side, covering me when the winds picked up and offering his hand whenever I stumbled. I felt cared for, protected, and not just in that moment, but in every moment we spent together.

That evening, as the sun dipped below the horizon, I found myself thinking more deeply about Rudhvik. He had shown me what it meant to feel valued, not just as a woman, but as a person worth cherishing. It was a rare kind of care, the kind that wasn't transactional, but unconditional. I felt myself warming to him in ways I hadn't anticipated, and I found myself thinking Maybe it's time to let go of the past. Maybe it's time to give him a chance.

The decision to move forward with Rudhvik had been a quiet battle within me. Each step felt like I was walking on a tightrope, the past stretching behind me like a chasm I couldn't cross, its echoes still loud in my mind. It wasn't that I didn't feel the pull of Rudhvik's sincerity, it was undeniable. But every time I allowed myself to inch closer to him, the shadows of the past would rush in, clawing at my heart, reminding me of the love I had lost. I was afraid. Afraid that no matter how much I wanted to open up, I might never fully escape the ghost of Dhruva.

Every moment with Rudhvik was a gift, but it also felt like a test. Could I truly let go of the man I had loved so deeply? Could I trust my heart again? His tenderness, his quiet understanding of these things made me feel safer than I had in years, yet I still couldn't quite shake the feeling that something was missing, that part of me was holding back.

But there was something in Rudhvik's eyes. His unwavering patience, the way he cared for me without ever asking for anything in return. He wasn't trying to replace Dhruva, and maybe, just maybe, that's what made him different. His love didn't come with the weight of comparison. It came with acceptance, with a promise that, no matter what, I didn't have to go through this alone. The possibility of healing had never seemed so real.

And so, with trembling resolve, I decided to take a step forward. To *finally* shed the old wounds that had clung to me like unwanted baggage, the ones I had carried for so long, so heavy, that I wasn't even sure what it felt like to move without them.

I planned something special for him, a surprise, something that was mine to give, to offer from a place that had once been too closed off. I wanted him to see the pieces of me that had been reluctant to show themselves, and I wanted him to know how deeply I was beginning to feel for him.

The evening of my surprise arrived, and the air in the apartment felt different and charged, as though the walls themselves knew what was about to unfold. I had transformed the place, dimming the lights, setting candles around the room to create a warmth that felt intimate, inviting. The scent of his favorite non-veg meal hung in the air, comforting and familiar. And as I stood there, waiting, dressed in a soft pink bodycon dress that clung to my body in a way that made me feel both vulnerable and exhilaratingly alive, my nerves were a storm inside me. I was terrified, and yet, there was something else, something soft, growing.

This wasn't just about the surprise. It wasn't just about the candles or the food or the way the apartment felt different. It was about letting go about taking that final step away from the shadows of the past and into something new, something I didn't fully understand but was willing to give a chance. To give *him* a chance.

When Rudhvik walked through the door, his eyes immediately found mine. The surprise was evident on his face, but it was his gaze, the way it softened, the way he took me in that stole my breath away. His confusion mixed with curiosity, making me laugh nervously. "Surprise!" I exclaimed, the words a little breathless, betraying the nervousness I couldn't quite shake. But then, as I watched his reaction, his eyes lighting up with joy, that simple, sincere smile spreading across his face, I felt my chest tighten with something I couldn't quite name. Maybe it was hope.

I motioned for him to change into something comfortable, and he compiled without hesitation. As I waited for him, my heart was beating so loudly in my chest I thought it might give me away. When he returned, I took a deep breath and led him to the center of the room, where I asked him to close his eyes. His brow furrowed in confusion, but he trusted me. There was no question in the way he followed my lead. I knelt, my heart hammering in my chest, my hands trembling as I held the small velvet box, the most vulnerable piece of myself I had ever offered.

"Rudhvik," I whispered, my voice trembling with the weight of everything I couldn't say. "Will you be mine?"

When he opened his eyes, I saw tears shimmer in his gaze. And in that moment, the world seemed to fall away. The tightness in my chest, the doubts, the fears all vanished in the quiet stillness between us. His hands trembled as he reached for me, his voice thick with emotion as he lifted me up, pulling me close.

"Yes," he said, his voice hushed, filled with awe. "Yes, I'll love to be yours forever."

The world around us faded. There was no past, no sorrow, no baggage. Just us. The kiss he placed on my forehead was tender, his lips warm and soft. But then, as if savoring every second, he kissed me on the lips, deep and slow, as though we were both claiming this moment, this new beginning. It was a kiss that held everything: the moments we'd shared, the unspoken understanding, the hope for everything that could be.

We celebrated with a quiet dinner, the soft hum of music in the background, but it was the slow dance that followed that truly marked the shift in my heart. His hands were gentle on my waist, his movements deliberate, each step measured, as if he was afraid to let go of the moment. But I was afraid of the past, afraid of opening myself up.

Yet, in his arms, it felt right. It felt like we were finally beginning to understand what was happening between us, something real, something beautiful. I nestled my head against his chest, feeling the steady beat of his heart, stronger than the turmoil inside me. It was like his heartbeat was a metronome, guiding me into the future, into this love that I had spent so long running from.

The night slipped away, not with a sense of urgency, but with the slow, deliberate unfolding of something new. It wasn't easy. It wasn't seamless. It wasn't a switch I could flip. But with every movement, with every breath we shared, I felt myself opening up to him in a way I hadn't thought possible.

And as we danced, I finally let go. Let go of the fear, of the past, of the old wounds I had carried for so long. They had no place here anymore, not in this new chapter we were writing together. In Rudhvik's arms, I felt the weight lift from my chest. I felt free, but at the same time, unsure. The scars of the past weren't something I could simply erase, and I wasn't certain if I could ever fully let go of the ghosts that lingered. Yet, in this moment, with him gentle, patient, and steady I dared to hope. I dared to believe that maybe, healing was possible. And that, despite the uncertainty, I could find peace in this love, a love that was still unfolding, still growing.

I let my wings shed away, ready to soar into the unknown. With him.

Six

Petals That Won't Regrow Again

The days after our intimate conversation were laced with silence, a weight between us that neither of us could ignore. It had been a week since the conversation, where Rudhvik, with all his tenderness and patience, had spoken openly about his desires. He hadn't brought it up again, but the unspoken tension between us was impossible to miss. It was like a quiet undercurrent in our once seamless relationship.

That Sunday, we had both decided to spend the day at home, enjoying each other's company after a week of busy schedules. We were cocooned in the warmth of the apartment, the sunlight filtering softly through the windows, casting a golden glow on everything it touched. The peacefulness of the moment was perfect. We laughed at silly jokes, shared stories from the past, and simply enjoyed the comfort of one another's presence.

Rudhvik, with his usual playfulness, kept pulling me close, teasing me with little affectionate gestures. His kisses, light at first, grew more intense as the afternoon wore on. We both sought comfort in each other, but somewhere in the back of my mind, I felt a knot tighten. There was an undercurrent I couldn't shake the conversation, the pressure, the expectations he had voiced so sincerely, yet so pointedly.

It wasn't that I didn't care for Rudhvik I did, more than I could explain but I wasn't sure I was ready. I believed in soulful love. The kind that transcends physical touch, that connects hearts before bodies. My past had left me cautious, scarred in ways I wasn't always willing to acknowledge. My relationship with Dhruva had taught me that love could be a beautiful, messy thing, but it also taught me that it could be fragile. When he cheated on me, I felt like my whole world shattered my trust, my beliefs about love and intimacy, all broken. The emotional scars were still there, and no matter how much I cared for Rudhvik, the fear of losing him, of making the wrong decision, was like a constant shadow hanging over me.

As Rudhvik's lips moved along my neck, tracing familiar paths that had once made me feel safe, I felt the familiar warmth of his touch but also the rising sense of unease in my chest. There was a desperation in his caresses, a hunger that wasn't there before, a shift I couldn't ignore. I pulled back slightly, just enough to look into his eyes, to see that they weren't just filled with affection but with something deeper, something that felt like expectation.

"I'm not ready," I whispered, my voice barely audible, but it was enough.

He froze for a moment, his eyes searching mine, trying to understand, and then, with a deep breath, he spoke softly, gently though I could hear the edge of frustration in his tone.

"Aadhvita, you're mine now," he said, his voice low, filled with something that felt both tender and serious. "Intimacy... it's a part of a relationship. It's not just about the physicality, but about being vulnerable with each other, sharing parts of ourselves we've never shared with anyone else. And if you don't want to, I won't force you. I respect your decision... But how long do you think I can control this need, this urge? I can't keep pretending that everything is fine when a part of me isn't... fulfilled. I need to know, Aadhvita. I need you to be mine in every way."

His words hung in the air between us, thick and heavy. I could feel the weight of them, the vulnerability he was offering me. It wasn't just about the act itself it was about his feelings, his expectations, and the deep emotional connection he had with me. But in that moment, it felt like an emotional tug-of-war inside me. I was torn between my fear and my affection for him. The idea of intimacy had always been so intertwined with love for me, and here

I was, standing on the precipice of something I wasn't entirely ready for.

His eyes softened, seeing the struggle in mine. "Please, just think about it. I'm not trying to rush you, Aadhvita. Just don't let this build up into something that drives us apart."

I nodded, my throat tight. "I need some time, Rudhvik... I'm not sure."

He kissed my forehead gently. "Take all the time you need. I'm not going anywhere."

But that night, as I lay in bed, the silence felt suffocating. Rudhvik had stayed on his side of the bed, quiet and respectful of my space, but I could feel the ache in his chest from across the room. And I could feel my own heart beating fast, too faster than usual. I closed my eyes, trying to sleep, but the pain of my indecision gnawed at me. I thought about what he had said about love and expectations, about the gap between us that I couldn't fill.

I cried. I cried not because I didn't love him, but because I feared losing him. The thought of him walking away because I couldn't meet his needs because I wasn't ready for this next step felt unbearable. And in the darkness of that night, I found myself wondering Is it worth risking everything to hold onto something that might slip through my fingers?

The tears flowed freely as I realized the depth of my love for him. The fear of losing him was so powerful it threatened to swallow me whole. I lay in the bed, alone with my thoughts, until exhaustion finally took over.

The next day, Rudhvik didn't press the issue. He remained as gentle as ever, respecting my space. I could see in his eyes that he had accepted my hesitation, but there was something about the way he looked at me that spoke volumes. The silence between us wasn't filled with resentment it was filled with a longing his quiet hope that one day, I would be ready.

It took a week for me to come to terms with what had happened. I couldn't stop thinking about the conversation. I couldn't stop thinking about him. Every time I saw him, I could feel the pull between us, the unspoken question hanging in the air. He was so patient, so understanding, but I knew he couldn't keep holding back forever. Neither could I.

At last, one evening as we were sitting on the couch, I replied, "Yes, Rudhvik," in a tremulous whisper, "I'm ready."

A mixture of relief and delight softened his gaze. He was very excited, and I wanted to be happy for him too, but I can't because I firmly believe in emotional connection without lust, where one longs for a single glimpse of their loved one; for them, holding hands is the sign of love. I've never been in a situation like that before, and every time I've been with someone I love, One side of my mind is fighting my emotions, and I don't want to get physically involved with anyone, not even the person I love.

Because if someone loves me, they will love me the way I am, without changing me into someone I never even wanted to be. But more than anything, my fear of losing Rudhvik made me so weak that I made the decision against my will, betraying my own beliefs. I said yes in the hopes that perhaps Rudhvik would stay with me forever and have no reason to leave, just like Dhruva did because I never engaged in a physical relationship with him. I can't afford to lose Rudhvik because I'm emotionally weak, but this same fear drove me to do something I'll never be able to forgive. I decided to compromise myself in the hopes that Rudhvik would never abandon me since I couldn't bear to lose him. With a heavy heart, I consented to have an intimate relationship with him.

I hesitated for a moment, but then Rudhvik stopped and whispered, "I'll never leave you Aadhvita, I love you to the moon and back." I smiled, trying to believe what he was saying, and then I gave him a gentle, soft kiss in return. When Rudhvik stood up and left me up by my thighs, locking our lips, he took me to the bedroom and carefully placed me on the bed without breaking our kiss. Rudhvik is slowly moving down towards my neck and pressing his lips against my skin. My eyes were closed because my heart was racing swiftly and I was breathing too quickly from the strange sensation and anxiety. Then, Rudhvik stopped and looked directly into my eyes, saying, "You are too cute, Aadhvita." I gave him a perplexed look, and he sat down and opened his t-shirt. For a brief moment, my eyes were frozen because I couldn't take my eyes off his curvy yet sharp body, which had muscles that were clearly visible. I felt a strange need to touch him, and my body became electrified. I bit my lower lips to symbolize a new need for Rudhvik's body and the desire for his closeness.

I couldn't believe my thoughts; this new sight of me that I had never seen before made my body tingle. I couldn't stop, so I put my hands on his lips and began to trace every inch of his body slowly upward and downward. Rudhvik then took my hand and wrapped it around his waist, kissed my chin slowly, moved to my neck, and then pulled my blue oversized t-shirt up, exposing my stomach and my white plain bra. I quickly tried to cover myself to prevent Rudhvik from making me half-naked, but he stopped me, saying, "I'm yours and you are mine; don't worry, I'm here to cover you with my body you don't need clothes, baby." I simply nod in obedience, and then Rudhvik gets lost in my body once more, kissing my belly and making me groan a little with pleasure. I'm discovering the romance, and now that we're both naked, Rudhvik sucks one tits while pressing the other, and I'm wrapped in my legs around his waist. My hands are still busy tracing his back and then his butts squeezing.

The moment gets more intense when Rudhvik takes the precaution out from under his pillow, saying he had brought it for this very moment. However, his need was at that moment, so he quickly put it on and began kissing my feet, slowly moving up to my inner thighs. I grabbed his hairs with both of my hands and went out of the pleasure of the kiss, and he gently forced himself into me this time. I felt a sharp pain that was unbearable, and I let out a soft scream because of the ache.

Then Rudhvik grasped both my wrists and gazed up into my eyes. It was a little unpleasant at first, but don't worry, you will eventually come to appreciate it. Then, a little too hastily, he forced himself and kissed my lips. I was unable to stop my nail from scratching his back whenever he moved. All the arteries and veins in my body were on fire. After a while, Rudhvik groans in pleasure and whispers, "Baby, you are too good. I love you." His eyes are wide and glistening a little teary, and so are mine, reflecting both pleasure and pain. I want more of him than this back and forth. I can feel something in my stomach, not discomfort, but a portion of him leaving his pleasurable essence in me forever. He lay on my bust and I stroked the back of his hair, saying, "I love you, Rudhvik, please don't ever leave me, my voice full of fear and anxiety, Rudhvik moved to lie next to me, enveloped me in his arms, and murmured, "Never, I promise," staring into my eyes then he kissed me on the forehead with assurance, admiration, love, and affection, as he held me, Rudhvik fell asleep, and I kept staring at his composed and calm face while my mind was racing with worries about what would happen if he left me, among other unfavorable thoughts.

After an hour of restful sleep, I got up and began getting dressed when Rudhvik abruptly woke up and gave me a back embrace. His face looked young and vibrant, and then he said, "Let's take a bath first," and took my hand, leading me to the bathroom. I felt a sense of uncertainty at first. But what happened next was completely unexpected. He began to clean me so gently and calmly, scrubbing me with a tenderness that wasn't needy or rushed. His actions were a clear reflection of pure care and concern. He wasn't just cleaning me, he was caring for me like I was the most delicate thing, like a little baby. In that moment, I began to feel an overwhelming sense of being valued, cherished, and loved.

As he cleansed me, I felt an emotional shift inside me. His quiet, selfless care made me feel more important than ever. It wasn't about physical attraction but the deep, unspoken connection between us. After the bath, he held my hand as he guided me back to the room. I was all dry, feeling so fresh and cared for, and he helped me put on my clothes and style my hair. Every little gesture every tender touch spoke volumes. It wasn't just about dressing me; it was about showing me that I was worth the effort.

At that moment, I couldn't help but fall for him even harder. I felt myself completely surrendering to him emotionally. His presence, his gentle care, and the way he made me feel like I was the most important thing in the world overwhelmed me in the best possible way. I let myself fall into him, allowing his fragrance to completely take over my senses, and for that brief moment, I felt as if I was part of something eternal. It wasn't just his scent, it was his essence, and I felt like it had claimed a piece of my soul.

In surrendering to him, I didn't feel weak or dependent. Instead, I felt deeply valued, treasured, and understood. There was a quiet, profound peace in knowing that I could trust him so fully. His love was not a demand, but a gift, and in that moment, I allowed myself to accept it completely. I knew that this connection between us was something deeper than anything I had ever experienced before something that would last a lifetime, perhaps even beyond that.

As the moments passed, I felt a deep sense of peace and warmth wash over me, but with it, a flicker of fear began to grow quietly in the back of my mind. I couldn't help but wonder, what if this wasn't as real for him as it felt for me? What if all this tenderness, all this care, was just a fleeting moment? What if Rudhvik would leave me, just like others had before? The thought of losing this connection, of losing him, made my heart ache in a way I couldn't explain.

I watched him for a second, trying to steady myself, as he continued to care for me with such devotion. His touch was so gentle, his smile so reassuring, but that tiny voice inside me couldn't help but whisper, "What if he doesn't feel the same way? What if one day, all of this is gone?" It was an insecurity I hated feeling, but it was there, gnawing at my heart.

What if I was too vulnerable, too open? What if I was allowing myself to fall too deeply, too quickly, and it would only hurt in the end? The fear of being abandoned, of being left behind when I had let myself become so completely attached to him, felt overwhelming.

But then, I reminded myself of what was happening at that moment. Rudhvik hadn't given me any reason to doubt him, in fact he was here with me now, holding my hand, making me feel like I mattered. I had to fight against that voice of insecurity, the voice that told me not to let go completely, not to surrender fully because I might get hurt.

Despite the fear, I couldn't deny the connection we shared. His presence was a balm for the uncertainty that clung to my thoughts. But still, the fear lingered, quiet but persistent, reminding me of past pains and disappointments. What if this time, I let myself believe too much, and it shattered in my hands?

I glanced at him again, looking into his eyes, hoping to find reassurance there. But inside, I was battling the fear of being vulnerable of allowing myself to fully believe in something so precious, yet fragile. Deep down, I knew I had to trust him, trust this moment, and trust myself to let go of the past. But the fear still clung to me, like a shadow, as I allowed myself to fall deeper into his care, wondering how long this beautiful moment could last, and whether it would ever truly be mine.

Seven

Uncovering the Unknowns

The days seemed to fly by when I was with Rudhvik. The chemistry between us was undeniable, growing stronger with each passing moment. His affection toward me was so much more than I could have ever imagined. Every touch, every word, every smile spoke of something deeper, something real. It wasn't just that he cared for me, but there was a tenderness in the way he showed it. Sometimes, I found myself marveling at how effortlessly he made me feel special, like I was the only person in his world. But there was always a sense of curiosity about him, a mystery that he never fully unveiled.

One day, just as I was settling into a quiet afternoon, my phone rang. It was Rudhvik, calling from his office. He had a surprise for me, and his voice had that familiar excitement I had come to recognize.

"Get ready, Aadhvita. I want to celebrate my salary day with you. We're going out on a date tonight," he said, the warmth in his tone lighting up my entire being. I could almost hear the smile in his voice.

A sense of anticipation swept over me. It was rare for Rudhvik to plan something so thoughtful, so I made sure to get ready, dressing in my favorite sea-green off-shoulder mini floral dress paired with casual white sneakers. I had always felt a little self-conscious in my more casual outfits, especially around someone like Rudhvik who had such a presence. But tonight was different. Tonight, I felt his care in every word and every gesture.

When we arrived at the venue, I was taken aback by the sheer beauty of the restaurant. The classic rooftop décor was nothing short of magnificent. A royal theme domiAadhvitaed the space, with golden chandeliers casting a soft glow over the tables, velvet curtains creating an intimate atmosphere, and the cool night air blending perfectly with the warmth of the setting. The view of the city skyline was breathtaking, and it felt like a dream. Yet, something about the evening felt off, though I couldn't quite put my finger on it.

Rudhvik, ever the charmer, held my hand as we were led to our table. His smile was radiant, his touch comforting, and for a brief moment, I allowed myself to relax into the beauty of the night. This was our time, a celebration of the small victories in our lives, and I couldn't wait to enjoy it with him. But as soon as the food arrived, everything seemed to shift.

The waiter set the plates down with professional grace, but when Rudhvik tasted the dish, I could immediately tell something was wrong. His face tightened, his eyes narrowed, and his voice rose, sharp with frustration.

"Excuse me!" he snapped, his tone harsh. "This is unacceptable. The food is cold, and it tastes like it's been sitting here for hours. What kind of service is this?"

I froze, my heart racing. The waiter, clearly taken aback, apologized and tried to explain, but Rudhvik wasn't hearing it. His eyes locked onto the manager as he approached, his words cutting through the air like a knife. "I came here to enjoy a meal, not to throw my money away on this... rubbish. Fix it, or I'm leaving." His tone was demanding, imperious, and I could see the discomfort in the manager's face.

A sense of discomfort settled deep within me, one I couldn't shake. I looked around the restaurant, aware of the gazes of other diners, and I couldn't help but feel embarrassed. The kindness I had always known in Rudhvik was buried beneath layers of impatience, and it left me feeling small, unimportant. The scene felt unnecessary, excessive, and I began to wonder if he even understood how his behavior was affecting me, let alone the staff who were just doing their jobs. His words were harsh, too sharp for the situation, and it made me feel so awkward.

I couldn't bear to stay there any longer, not with the tension hanging between us. I pushed my plate aside, my appetite gone, and stood up quickly, my chair scraping noisily against the floor. "I'm leaving," I said, my voice quiet, but firm. I couldn't stay in a place where the discomfort of the situation overshadowed everything.

"Aadhvita, wait," Rudhvik called after me, his voice laced with frustration, but I couldn't stay. I was too upset, too disappointed. The discomfort was more than I could handle, and without saying another word, I walked out of the restaurant, leaving behind the unfinished meal, the unsaid words, and the painful tension.

The drive home was heavy with silence, the car feeling colder than it ever had before. I couldn't bring myself to look at him, my thoughts swirling in a haze of confusion and disappointment. Rudhvik seemed lost in his own world, though I could tell he wasn't pleased with how the evening had turned out. Neither was I.

Then, as if to break the weight of the silence, I made a spontaneous decision. We didn't need an expensive dinner or a lavish venue to enjoy each other's company. What we needed was something simple, something genuine. I pulled the car over at a roadside tea stall, the familiar scent of chai wafting through the air as we stepped out. The little shop, tucked away at the corner of the street, had an unpretentious charm that made me feel at ease.

As we sipped the tea, I tried to shake off the feeling of awkwardness that clung to me. But then, a girl passed by the stall, and I saw Rudhvik's gaze follow her. A wave of insecurity flooded through me, sharp and sudden. Was I not enough? Why was he looking at her?

I couldn't stop myself from pinching his shoulder playfully, trying to mask the jealousy with a teasing smile. "What? Pretty girl, yeah?"

He blinked, clearly caught off guard. "What?" he asked, his voice light with confusion.

I nodded toward the girl, but my voice faltered, my feelings betraying me. "Pretty girl, huh?"

Rudhvik chuckled, a mischievous glint in his eyes. "Jealous, hmm?" he teased, his voice playful.

"No way," I snapped, trying to cover my insecurity with a feigned attitude. But deep down, I couldn't ignore the tightening of my chest. Was I still his priority?

He leaned in closer, brushing a strand of hair behind my ear, his voice soft but filled with certainty. "Not as pretty as you are, my girl," he said, his words sweeping away the doubt in my heart.

I rolled my eyes, teasing him in return. "You liar," I said, a playful disgust on my face, but the truth of his words settled in my chest, making my heart flutter.

Without hesitation, Rudhvik pulled me closer, his lips pressing against my forehead in a soft kiss. "I mean it," he whispered, his breath warm against my skin. "You are the one I see. Always."

It was in that moment, as I felt his arms around me and his warmth seep into me, that I realized something profound. He wasn't just my boyfriend; he was my partner in every sense. He wasn't afraid to love me openly, to show the world that I was his. And in that, there was a strength I had never seen in anyone else.

I looked up at him, my heart swelling with love, gratitude, and a deep sense of peace. He was mine. And I was his. And that was all that mattered.

When we finally made it home, I couldn't shake the sense of disappointment that still lingered. The evening had been ruined, and I couldn't stand the idea that Rudhvik had gone without a proper meal because of me. I needed to make things right.

As he changed clothes, I quickly ordered his favorite margarita pizza from Domino's. When it arrived, I set the dining table with a bottle of wine, two glasses, and everything I thought would help lift his spirits. I wanted to show him that even though the night hadn't gone as planned, it didn't mean it was beyond saving.

By the time Rudhvik came back into the room, I had everything set up. His eyes lit up with excitement as he took in the scene. "What's all this?" he asked, his tone surprised but full of appreciation.

I couldn't help but smile, feeling a wave of pride wash over me. "I wanted to make it up to you," I said, stepping forward to pull him into my arms. I kissed his chin softly, my heart in my throat. "I'm sorry for ruining the date."

He smiled, gently lifting my chin and meeting my eyes. "It's not your fault," he said, his voice steady but filled with warmth. "Don't blame yourself." He kissed me then, pulling me up onto my toes, his lips pressing against mine in a tender, reassuring kiss.

When we sat down together, our glasses of wine in hand, I felt the weight of the night begin to lift. We clink our glasses together, and I felt the tension finally ease. We ate the pizza together, talking about everything and nothing, and for the first time that evening, I could breathe again.

But as we ate, something was still on my mind. I wanted to know more about Rudhvik, the man beneath the surface, the one who held everything in.

"Vik," I said, my voice soft, "I want to know you more. I want to know the real you."

He looked at me, his face unreadable for a moment. Finally, with a sigh, he agreed. "Okay, I'll tell you a few things. But only because you're my partner, and you deserve to know

As he spoke, the walls I had never known existed came down. He told me about his addiction to drugs and alcohol, his need for escape, the loneliness he had felt growing up. He spoke of the emotional scars left by his parents, of the years spent away from them in a hostel, trying to navigate life without the support he so desperately needed.

Tears welled up in his eyes as he spoke, and for the first time, I saw him for who he truly was—a man broken by the past, yet still trying to find his way. His pain, his vulnerability, shattered everything I thought I knew about him.

"You won't understand," he said, his voice heavy with emotion, "because you had a dream childhood. You had your parents with you."

I swallowed hard, my heart breaking for him. "Maybe not," I whispered, "but I understand that you need someone now. I understand that you need love, too."

As I held him close, I felt a deep desire to protect him, to love him in a way that would heal the wounds he had carried for so long. I kissed him gently, promising silently that I would never let him go. That I would be the one to help him heal.

That night, as he finally fell asleep in my arms, I whispered a silent vow to myself: I would love him unconditionally, without hesitation, and give him all the happiness he had been deprived of for so long. I would love him wholeheartedly, for everything he was and everything he could be.

And I would never let go.

Eight

Reflection of Reality

It's been more than a week since Rudhvik left for his hometown near Indore for a family function, and I'm alone at home. It was hard for me to survive even a minute without him because I'm so reliant on him, but by God's grace, he didn't let me feel alone despite our distance from one another. He continued to text and video call me occasionally and update me on his days, and he didn't stop caring for me even though he was too busy with his family. If I forget, he still finds time for me, which is very mature and sensible of him; he is truly a perfect partner.

One night when Rudhvik called. I woke up and answered my phone, but his voice shook me since he was intoxicated. He said, "I miss you, honey. I want you so badly." I replied, "I miss you too, Vik. Is everything okay?" He replied, "Aadhvita, I want to fuck you. I love you, baby." His voice was slurred by drink. He stated all of this in front of his cousins, and the agony and hurt make my body go numb. His words pierced my soul like a sharp sword. What he said to me is intolerable; I'm boiling with rage, and my eyes are watering like tap water. The universe has turned upside down, the room is bursting, and I feel like throwing up. I shouted, "Dare you out of your mind, or what, Rudhvik?" I can't believe that you would humiliate me in this way and disrespect our relationship and space. Rudhvik, you didn't deserve my trust; you are a cheap pervert, and I shouldn't have trusted you. You broke my heart and my trust; why did you do that to me? My voice is shaking as I snooze, and I'm crying too much. When Rudhvik realized what he had done, he immediately apologized to me, but I couldn't take it any longer. I told him, "I hate you, get lost, and never even call me again ever." Rudhvik still apologized, so I ended the call. In my dark room, I yelled out loud, regretting trusting Rudhvik and losing my innocence to someone who just saw me as a toy. My entire world was trembling from the harm Rudhvik had caused, as well as from the unbreakable pain and rage. How could he do that? I grieved all night long, blaming myself and feeling guilty, as if I trusted and loved him too much and let him jeopardize everything. He quickly took away my dignity, treating me like a piece of trash that can be used and denigrated anywhere, at any time. At the moment, I felt like I had lost myself and had given up everything for someone who didn't appreciate me. Somehow, the entire night is spent in anguish and tears.

That evening, Rudhvik contacted me numerous times, but I didn't answer.

Later in the evening, I pulled myself together and mustered the strength to get ready. When I looked at my face, the glow had gone and the dark circles were clearly visible, giving the impression that I was dead. Nevertheless, I summoned the courage and got ready, and that day I worked extremely hard to ignore the pain I was feeling inside. Living solely on water and without eating anything made me feel as though my appetite had also died.

However, at about eight o'clock in the evening, I called Dhruva, whom I had been neglecting for about a month. Dhruva answered my call after only one ring, as if he was waiting for me, and he said, "Hy Aadhvita," in a kind manner. I responded, "Hye being fake." As I asked him, "Where are you, Dhruva? He said, "In your city," and without pausing, he asked me out for a drink and said he would pick me up by his car. I didn't respond for a moment because I was running towards Rudhvik, wondering how he would react, but without thinking, I said, "Okay, see you tonight," and hung up. I dressed really well in blue jeans, a grey oversized t-shirt with loose hair, and white sneakers, then I put the laptop on the side table in my room and sat on the couch waiting for Dhruva. He arrived to pick me up after 30 minutes, I promptly locked the apartment and went to the parking lot. I saw Dhruva smile and sit in the car. Dhruva said, "You seem exhausted,

Aadhvita. What happened?" I said nothing; perhaps it was because of my workload that I lied and pretended to smile. He nodded and went on to apologize for hurting me and how much I mean to him while driving a car. I was absorbed in Rudhvik's thoughts because he hadn't called me since the morning and was thinking about the previous night's incident. and repeatedly inflicting pain on myself, Dhruva called my name a bit too loudly to bring me back to reality. He then said, "Where are you lost?" I replied, "Nowhere." He then drove to a wine shop and brought us a bottle of red wine, saying, "We can drink inside the car if you feel comfortable." I nodded in agreement, and he parked the car near the empty garden in Noida, though I'm not sure where. He then opened the bottle of wine, and we shared it since it's too strong to drink it all at once. I looked at Dhruva, who was wearing a blue denim shirt and smoky-colored jeans, and he looked nice, but not as intelligent and attractive as my Rudhvik, I thought. He finished his drink, handed it to me to take a sip, and held my hand. He then said, "I regret losing you because you are the only one weep for me." I tried to turn away, but he pulled me in and held me picking me up and placing me on his lap. I tried to release his grip, but what he said next made me reconsider. Tell me who you see, Aadhvita, and when I kiss you. only to temporarily take away both your and my suffering? I was certain that I wouldn't see anything because, at that very moment I hate Rudhvik because he betrayed my trust and left me broken, I froze and just nodded without saying anything. Dhruva then started kissing me, and he kissed me hard before holding me close and encircling me in his arm. I grabbed back of Dhruva's hair and managed to create a gap, and when he kissed me, I saw a clear image of Rudhvik in front of my eyes. I don't know how it's even conceivable that the touch I was experiencing was so uncomfortable; my body recognized Rudhvik's and a stranger's touch, making me feel uneasy. This has never happened to me before. Dhruva is the person I used to love, but my body is just not acknowledging or accepting his touch, and therefore declares him a stranger. Dhruva then moved further down, pushing my bust, and I stopped him. He apologized, and then he asked, "Who do you see?" When I replied, "No one," Dhruva gave me a serious look. When I nod, he said same here he added, before asking if I would let him touch me a bit further and making a remark about how enormous my bust was. I couldn't figure it out, so I didn't respond. Dhruva went on, "Aadhvita, please don't think that I'm using you or anything like that." "Yes," I said, "I understand. I'm merely attempting to console you. "Okay, let's do that," Dhruva responded when I indicated that I wanted to go home. When I went back to my seat, Dhruva grinned and said, "Thank you," which seemed like a victory. I felt like I was being taken advantage of, but I couldn't react because Rudhvik and Dhruva exploit me in their own way, shattering my soul, and the kiss I just had makes it obvious to me that Rudhvik is the one I can't live without because not only does my body become bound to him, but my spirit does as well. If he breaks me, I'll take it, but, aside from Rudhvik, I can't bear to be touched by anybody else again. I want to thank Dhruva for this realization, as well as for his eerie kiss and awkward moment.

The body has memories of its own, and I discovered that it acknowledged the touch of the person who makes you feel at home.

I opened my shoes as soon as I got home and hurried to the bathroom, where I puked and scrubbed myself so hard that my lips began to bleed. I felt disgusted, and I cried and screamed, wanting Rudhvik to take me in his arms and make me feel safe and needed. I then checked my phone and called Rudhvik. Even though I'm still upset, I can't allow anyone else to touch me and I will never forgive him. Yes, I'm sacrificing my dignity once more, but I can't picture anyone using me. Only Rudhvik has the right to touch me.I contacted him three times, but his phone is off. I became anxious.

After two days, I'm still feeling really nervous and depressed. I don't know if Rudhivik felt the same way about me, so how could he leave me like this? He is aware of how much I worried and overanalyzed his absence.

I eat nothing but oats out of worry because I'm too easily distracted by these thoughts.

On the evening of the third day, I received an unknown call that I had been ignoring the night before, but this time I answered it. It was Vedhit, a friend of Rudhvik's from college, and he informed me that Rudhvik had an accident yesterday, which meant that after our argument, I instantly thought it was a joke until, Vedhit sent me the pictures of Rudhvik lying in a hospital bed, his shoulder badly fractured, my heart sank. He told me there were multiple fractures, and guilt immediately consumed me. This time, it wasn't just guilt, it was suffocating. I could hardly breathe. My emotions were a chaotic whirlwind, and I needed someone to turn to. That someone was my mother.

I hadn't been in frequent contact with her recently because I knew how easily she panicked, and I didn't want to worry her. She'd started to miss me, I could tell, but I kept my distance. However, this time, I decided I would call her, especially since I had planned to spend my birthday with her this year. She picked up the phone after a long silence, and her voice, full of warmth and relief, instantly brought me a sense of comfort.

"Finally, I hear your voice, my little girl," she said, and it was as if a gentle breeze of peace washed over me just from hearing her. But then, the dam broke. I couldn't hold back the tears anymore. The weight of everything crushed me, and I started to cry uncontrollably.

My mom immediately sensed something was wrong. "What happened, my girl? Why are you crying? Tell me, please." Her voice was filled with concern, but also that deep love that could heal anything.

Through my sobs, I managed to choke out the words, "Rudhvik... he met with an accident."

My mother's voice faltered for a moment, and I could hear her panic rising, but she quickly steadied herself. "Don't panic, sweetheart. Stay calm. Just pray to God. He'll be fine."

I felt her strength through the phone, as though her words alone could soothe the chaos inside me. My mother, though strong and full of life with a loud, commanding personality, was also deeply emotional, sensitive, and incredibly kind-hearted. Her soothing presence wrapped around me like a blanket, making me feel safe despite everything.

As we continued talking, she told me that Rudhvik had kept in touch with her, despite his shyness. He and I had been friends since school, and through our relationship, he had formed a bond with my family. It was something I had always found hard to believe Rudhvik was the type who kept to himself, not one to open up easily. But over time, he had managed to connect with my family, and that made me feel proud of him in a way I hadn't expected.

Slowly, the panic inside me began to fade, replaced by the calming effect of my mother's healing words. Her strength, her ability to remain composed, was a constant reminder of the warrior she was. I felt the tension ease from my shoulders, and though the situation was still difficult, I knew with her guidance, everything would eventually be okay.

I slowly pulled away from the phone call with my mom, the comfort of her voice lingering in my heart, but there was still a heavy knot in my chest. "Thank you, Mom. Take care of yourself. I'll call you again soon," I said, trying to steady my emotions.

"Same to you, my dear. Keep praying to God, and don't let sadness take over," she replied gently, her voice a balm to my soul.

I took a deep breath, forcing a small smile despite the tears that still lingered in my eyes. "Okay, Mom," I whispered before ending the call. But even as the phone clicked off, the emptiness of not having her physically with me at that moment made me ache. I missed her more than ever.

Needing to know more about Rudhvik's condition, I quickly typed a message to Vedhit, asking how he was doing. My phone buzzed with a video call, and my heart skipped a beat when I saw Vedhit's face on the screen.

He didn't waste time. He turned the camera, and there was Rudhvik, lying in a hospital bed. His face was pale, but his eyes... they were alive. He saw me, and a soft smile appeared on his lips, though it was tinged with a sadness that broke me inside. "I miss you," he said, his voice soft and raspy, a faint vulnerability in his words.

Tears welled up in my eyes, but I forced a smile through them. "I love you," I whispered back, my voice trembling, as I looked at him, my heart aching from everything that had happened.

Vedhit's voice interrupted the moment, and I realized his family had gathered around Rudhvik in the hospital room. A few moments later, Vedhit ended the call without informing me, his presence fading from the screen. But in that instant, I felt a weight lift from my chest, knowing Rudhvik was okay, at least for now. A sense of relief washed over me, though my heart still carried the burden of everything left unsaid.

A week passed, and Rudhvik was finally discharged from the hospital. But even though he was home, he was still bedridden for a while, recovering from the multiple fractures that had kept him in the hospital. Despite the pain and his limitations, we stayed in constant contact. Every day, he would video call me, apologizing for everything, the hurtful words, the disrespect, and, most painfully, for leaving me to face everything alone.

His apologies were sincere, but they didn't heal the wounds he'd caused. Still, in my heart, I knew living without him was more unbearable than holding onto the pain. It wasn't easy to forgive him, but in my soul, I knew we were meant to heal together.

Then, the day I had been waiting for finally came. Rudhvik was home, and he was in my arms again. But as much as I longed for this moment, a wave of nervousness washed over me. The joy of seeing him, of holding him close, was mingled with a fear that tightened around my chest. How could I tell him about what had happened with Dhruva? How would he react? Would he leave me once he found out? The thought gnawed at me, making my heart ache even more.

But even in the midst of that fear, there was a sense of joy and comfort in being near him again. The warmth of his body, the security of his presence softened the sharp edges of my anxiety, just a little.

I opened the door to find him standing there, looking so much like the man I had missed. I was wearing nothing but pajamas, an oversized t-shirt, and my hair in a messy bun. My face was still sleep-ridden from the morning fog, but none of that mattered. The moment I saw him, the world around me disappeared. I couldn't wait a second longer.

Without thinking, I rushed into his arms, jumping up to wrap my legs around him. He caught me effortlessly, and his lips met mine in a kiss that was deep, passioAadhvitae, and full of everything we had both been holding back. I felt a rush of warmth, of safety, and of longing all at once.

He broke the kiss briefly, but not before he kicked the door shut with his foot, keeping me close. I whispered against his lips, "Vik, I missed you."

He kissed my forehead, the tenderness in his touch making my heart swell. "I missed you too," he said softly, his words laced with sincerity. Slowly, he lowered me back down, placing me gently on the couch beside him.

He sat down next to me, pulling me into him, his hand cradling the back of my head. "Baby, I'm sorry for everything I said. For what I did. We'll talk about it later, I promise," he murmured, his voice filled with regret.

I closed my eyes for a moment, trying to calm the storm inside me. But in his arms, the weight of everything seemed to lessen. Still, there was something we needed to face. Something I needed to tell him. But not now.

"Let's go inside and sleep for a while," I suggested, my voice quiet but steady.

He looked at me with a playful glint in his eyes and gave me a mischievous wink. "You want to sleep? Or are you just trying to avoid talking?"

I smiled softly, my nerves fluttering. "We'll talk later. I just want to be with you now."

He grinned, lifting me in his arms again, and we walked into my room together, leaving the world outside for a moment. As soon as we were inside, I could feel the safety of his presence, but the unspoken words still lingered between us, waiting for the right moment.

I let the fear go for a while because I am so desperate for Rudhvik's embrace right now. Without wasting any time, I quickly removed my T-shirt and am now only wearing my plain black bra, allowing my half body to feel every inch of his skin as we indulge our energy together. Vik was astonished and delighted by my sudden action, so he opened his lime-colored plain t-shirt and leaped on the bed to wrap me around his arms. Vik then sucked my neck, leaving a mark, and moved to kiss my lips before biting my lower lips, making me crave more. He unhooked my bra and started pressing and sucking, one by one, making me moan with pleasure. He watched me closely, noticing how lost I was in the moment, enjoying every touch of him. He then kissed my lower belly, removing my pajama. In order to intensify the romance, he removed his pants. When he was wearing protection, I traced his collarbone. When he finished, I drew him in closer, moving slowly down and then up with each movement to trace his stomach and chest. Rudhvik was making noises for fun at the time, and I loved controlling his body and realizing that he was enjoying my touch and becoming more and more lustful for me. Then, he stopped me and continued to bite my inner thigh, delineating his territory, then he took off my black underwear and wrapped my legs around his waist, warning in a seductive tone, baby I'm Coming I can't help but laugh at him, baby. He looks up directly into my eyes, his brows raised, then looks down and gives me a gentle kiss on my feet. Then the time comes, he carefully forces himself inside of me, not wanting to hurt me, and my thighs shiver with pleasure. He keeps moving back and forth slowly this time, until I say, "Please, baby, please, move faster," and then he moves faster. My body wants to be filled with the love, memories, and vigor of Him, yes, only him. I let my desire free and let him ink my soul with his name declaring self that I only belong to Rudhvik, and the faster he moves, the more I need him. However, I felt a sharp pain inside, so I steamed and asked him to stop. He stopped right away and looked up to make sure I was okay. What happened, Aadhvita? Are you okay? I replied to Rudhvik, "Yes, my eyes are teary. He is now sitting and rushed his hand to wipe my tears and hug me, caressing softly. I'm sorry, baby, I hurt you." He seemed very anxious, and his eyes were filled with sorrow. "I'm sorry," he continued, "but it's okay, you didn't do it on purpose, so please don't feel bad." I then cupped his face through my hands and bit his upper lip, kissing me in return. He wrapped his tongue around mine, and I traced his back to see the marks I had made. Rudhvik paused and asked, "Why don't you close your eyes while kissing?"

I replied that I didn't know, and he asked me to explain. I told him that every time I closed my eyes, memories from the past began to haunt me, which made me afraid and made me assume that you would leave me too, Vik.

He remained motionless and continued to stare before kissing my forehead and saying, "Aadhvita, you must believe in me and my love for you." His look grew more solemn and intense with each sentence, so I asked him if he felt me today before he continued. I was moved by every word that came out of his mouth as I tried to shift the conversation. "Yes, Aadhvita, I'm happy with you. Don't worry, and don't ever compromise yourself just because of me." He just mastered the art of controlling me in every aspect, he has a profound awareness of my thoughts, needs, and desires, which, in my opinion, has both positive and negative aspects.

It's good that he understands me so well, but it's bad because he can exploit it.

After a moment of silence, I gently suggested, "Maybe you should take a bath. You must be exhausted." Rudhvik looked at me, nodding with a small smile, as if grateful for the simple care I was offering. He took my hand, leading me toward the bathroom, and without a word, he started to cleanse me with tenderness.

As he did, he kissed my forehead softly, and I couldn't help but wrap my arms around him. He didn't push me away, he welcomed me into his embrace, gently caressing my hair as we stood there together, the sound of water filling the air. It felt like a quiet, private moment, one where time slowed down just for us.

When he finally finished, he dried me off with a towel, his hands gentle and sure. He looked at me with a warm smile and said, "Go back to the room, I'll be there in a minute." I nodded, feeling a strange sense of calm wash over me, and left for the room.

I began to get dressed, pulling on my clothes slowly, but just as I was about to fasten my bra, Rudhvik rushed into the room. Without hesitation, he reached out, hooking the straps for me and helping me into it as if it was something natural. He stood there, wrapped only in a towel, and as he did, he whispered, "Baby, you're only mine." A smile tugged at my lips as I looked up at him. There was no doubt in my heart as I realized how deeply he meant it.

We were both finally ready, and we settled onto the bed, the softness of the sheets under us feeling like a comfort after everything that had happened. My thoughts drifted to the future, and with a sense of curiosity, I turned to him. "What about marriage? Kids? What's your plan for the future?"

Rudhvik's eyes lit up, and his voice was filled with joy. "I want to marry you, Aadhvita. And I really want to have kids with you. A daughter, especially."

I raised an eyebrow, intrigued. "Why a daughter?"

He smiled, a thoughtful expression crossing his face. "So I can make her the strongest woman. I want to show her that women don't have to be soft or weak, that they can't be broken easily. I want to change that idea, break the taboos."

His words touched me deeply, and I felt a wave of pride for him. The thought of him as a father, someone who would raise a daughter to be strong and unshakable, made my heart swell with admiration. How lucky was I to have such a wonderful man in my life? I could already picture him being a supportive, loving father.

We continued talking, the conversation flowing as we shared our hopes for the future. Rudhvik then asked me the same question, and I paused before responding. "I don't really believe in marriage," I said softly, my voice carrying the weight of my beliefs. "I don't think anything is permanent. As for kids... I'd rather adopt. There are so many children out there who need parents. I'd want to give them a home."

Rudhvik listened intently, his gaze soft and understanding. But as I spoke, I noticed his eyes begin to flutter, the exhaustion from the day catching up with him. His breathing slowed, and before I knew it, he was asleep beside me.

I leaned over and kissed his cheek gently, my lips brushing against his warm skin. With a content sigh, I nestled my head on his chest, the steady rhythm of his heartbeat soothing me. I let all my worries, all my tension, melt away. There was peace in his presence, in the comfort of his arms and for the first time in a long while, I let myself drift into sleep, feeling safe and loved.

Nine

Forever Embrace

The following morning, at the start of a new day, Rudhvik woke up early and made me a cup of coffee. He gently woke me with his beautiful smile and warm embrace, a moment that made me want to surrender completely to him. His unexpected gesture was a pleasant surprise, especially considering we are both known to be night owls. The fact that he made the effort to do this for me touched me deeply. As he sat beside me, he softly said, "Baby, you know how much I love you."

Before the day could fully unfold, he took a moment to apologize, his voice sincere. "I'm so sorry for hurting you with my words," he said. "I shouldn't have said those things. I was intoxicated, and I was missing you so much. I never meant to hurt you." As I listened, tears began to roll down my face. His words reminded me of the deep humiliation and disrespect I had felt when he had spoken so crudely in front of his brother. The words he used that day caused me immense pain. Deep down, I knew that forgiving him would mean compromising my self-respect, something no woman should ever have to do. I couldn't bear the thought of losing him, though. The idea of him leaving me was suffocating. I could barely breathe, and even though a part of me wanted to leave him to teach him a lesson, I knew I couldn't. I needed him, not because I loved him so deeply, but because I didn't know how to live without him.

In that moment, I gained a new understanding and immense respect for women who survive toxic relationships, who endure pain and abuse, whether physical, emotional, or verbal. I'm not saying my relationship is like that, but I now understand the strength it takes to forgive and continue despite being mistreated. Women who repeatedly choose to forgive, in the hope that one day their partner will change, deserve great respect. They prioritize love above all else, enduring abuse in the hope that their partner will eventually see their worth.

To those who call these women cowards, I disagree. They are fighters. They know their true selves and their love is stronger than any circumstances. What they don't yet realize is that they can only survive without their loved ones when they've learned to live without them. They try everything they can to save the relationship, and they only leave once they've given it their all. For those who believe a career is more important than a relationship, I say: learn to love, because no profession should ever come before the bond between two people who truly care for each other.

Relationships require compromise and sacrifice. If today I choose self-respect over the relationship, maybe tomorrow I'll have to compromise my choice, because people evolve and change. It's the nature of a healthy relationship: both partners need to be willing to change and grow. If they love each other, they will. And if not, time will reveal the truth because loyalty is costly, and everyone must pay for it.

After Rudhvik finished his apology, I felt ready to confess something to him. He was my man, and he needed to know what his actions had caused me. "Rudhvik, I have a confession to make," I said. His face shifted to one of curiosity, "What is it, Aadhvita? Please, tell me."

"I made a mistake after our fight," I said, unsure of how he would react. He leaned forward, intrigued. "What mistake?" he asked. "Please, tell me everything clearly."

"I'm afraid you'll be angry or leave me," I replied, voice shaking. He reassured me, saying he would neither get angry nor leave. "I promise," he added, his voice soft but steady.

So, I told him about the meeting with Dhruva, about how my body had not recognized his touch in a way that I hadn't expected. As I shared these details, my voice faltered, and my hands shook uncontrollably. Rudhvik, listening intently, didn't interrupt, but I could see the emotions swirling within him. When I finished speaking, he looked at me with hurt in his eyes and said, "Why did you hurt me, Aadhvita? You kissed your ex just because we had a fight?"

I corrected him gently. "It wasn't just a fight, Rudhvik. You disrespected me." I could see the disappointment and hurt in his eyes, and it made my heart ache. I reached for his hand, still trembling, as we sat facing each other on the bed. "Vik, I'm so sorry," I whispered.

He pulled me into a hug, holding me silently for a long moment. In his arms, I felt the tension release, and I could finally breathe again, reassured that he wasn't going anywhere. When he pulled back, he spoke again, his voice more serious than before. "We both made mistakes, but Aadhvita, what you did was not appropriate. Kissing your ex, especially after we had a fight, was not okay."

I nodded, my heart heavy with regret. "I promise I won't do it again," I said, my voice barely a whisper.

He smiled softly, then said, "I promise I won't hurt you again, Aadhvita." With those words, he kissed my forehead, and in that moment, a sense of peace washed over both of us.

I felt incredibly blessed at that moment. Rudhvik understood me, he saw me for who I truly was. Instead of being rude, aggressive, or walking away like so many others might have, he chose to stay. He knew that I belonged to him, soulfully and completely. And I could see that he realized the same thing. It was a rare gift, one that made me feel deeply loved and cared for.

Ten

Beyond Acceptance

A month had passed when one evening, Rudhvik called to remind me about a get-together I had almost forgotten. It was a school friends' meet-up, which we had planned a week before since most of our friends were in the city. Rudhvik told me that he would be coming directly from his office to the venue. Desi Vibe, a restaurant in Noida and he would wait for me there.

The evening was filled with the joyful noise of friends reconnecting, their voices blending together like a symphony of laughter and conversation. I walked into the restaurant, wearing a peach satin cut-out gown paired with white heels, my hair left loose. A warm sense of nostalgia flooded over me as I saw my old friends gathered around a large table. We were in Desi Vibe, the restaurant where we had chosen to meet, exuded a royal charm that instantly captivated my senses. The interior was an opulent fusion of modern elegance and traditional Indian aesthetics. Rich, golden accents adorned the walls, creating a luxurious yet inviting atmosphere, and the excitement in the air was palpable. But amidst the laughter and chatter, my eyes were immediately drawn to Rudhvik, who stood near the entrance. He looked as stunning as ever, dressed in a navy blue formal shirt and grey pants, waiting for me.

He had this innate ability to make me feel like I was the only person in the room, as though the world paused for just a second the moment I walked into it. His presence was magnetic, and tonight, he was about to show me why.

As we entered the restaurant together, Rudhvik didn't just casually follow behind me, like many others might have done. No, he was by my side, moving with me. His steps matched mine, his eyes never leaving me. It felt like everything else in the room blurred as he made sure I knew that I was the only one he cared about. As we reached the table, where my friends were already seated, my gaze immediately landed on Anvika. She was the one who had always had an undeniable crush on Rudhvik everyone knew it. I noticed her glancing at him with a subtle longing whenever he moved, her body language trying to catch his attention, hoping to spark something.

But Rudhvik... he remained entirely oblivious. In fact, I don't think he even noticed. His gaze was fixed on me. His eyes were focused solely on me, as though no one else even existed in his world.

I felt a flutter in my chest, a warmth spreading through me that only Rudhvik could bring. He was completely mine in that moment, and that truth made me feel cherished, seen, and above all, secure.

As we approached the table, Rudhvik didn't sit across from me as most would have expected; instead, he pulled a chair closer to his, making space for me right beside him. The gesture was simple yet deeply meaningful. It wasn't just about proximity; it was about closeness, about sharing that space with me and no one else. In that moment, it was as if the entire world faded into the background, and it was just the two of us, together.

Anvika, meanwhile, tried her best to get Rudhvik's attention. I could see her laughter ringing out a little louder than usual, her body subtly angling toward him, the way she leaned in when he spoke. But Rudhvik never once turned in her direction. He was engaged in our conversation, his focus entirely on me. He seemed to instinctively block out everything else. It was as though I had his full attention, and no one else mattered in that moment.

He wasn't just present physically, he was present with his heart. He opened the menu for me before I even had to ask, subtly guiding me through the choices. It was a simple act, but the tenderness of it made me feel so cared for. As I went to the restroom, he stood up immediately, opening the door for me, waiting for me to return with that same quiet strength, eyes scanning the room until they found me again. His patience, his attention was all directed at making sure I felt special, even in the busiest of moments.

When the food arrived, Rudhvik didn't just serve me; he took the time to lift a piece of food from his plate and offered it to me with his own hand, his touch gentle as he fed me. It was such a small thing, but it spoke volumes. The warmth in his eyes as he did it, the calm assurance in his movements made me realize that this was how love should feel. It wasn't grand gestures or declarations; it was in the quiet moments, in the simple acts of care. As he fed me, I felt like the most important person in the room, not because of attention from anyone else, but because Rudhvik's affection for me was so deep, so consuming, that it made everything else feel insignificant.

And still, Anvika's eyes were on us. But it didn't matter. Her longing glances, the way she positioned herself to draw attention but none of it reached me. Rudhvik's love for me was so apparent, so obvious in the way he treated me. It was as though his whole world was built around me, and I had the privilege of being in it.

His touch was possessive in the most tender way. As my hand rested on the table, his fingers casually brushed mine, then interlocked with them, as if to say, *This is where you belong.* And when I leaned in, his hand gently found the back of my head, caressing my hair with such tenderness, it felt like he was anchoring me in that moment, reminding me that I was his, and he was mine.

I had never experienced anything like this before. I had never known that love could be so quietly powerful, so beautifully consistent. I had always feared that love meant needing to be something I wasn't, but with Rudhvik, I didn't need to be anyone else. He loved me for exactly who I was. Every imperfection, every flaw, every part of me that I had once thought unworthy, he loved it all.

As the night continued, I found myself lost in the warmth of his presence. But there was a moment, just a small flicker, when my best friend Manav, who had always been like a brother to me, leaned in during a quiet conversation. Without thinking, he brushed his lips lightly against my cheek. It was a simple, friendly gesture, nothing more. But the moment he pulled away, I saw something shift in Rudhvik's expression. It was subtle, a slight tightening of his jaw, a quick flash of possessiveness in his eyes.

It wasn't anger. It wasn't jealousy. It was something deeper, a protective instinct, a quiet reminder to the world that I was his. Not in an oppressive way, but in the way someone holds onto something precious, something irreplaceable. Rudhvik's gaze met mine, and though he didn't say anything, the emotion in his eyes was clear: *I care for you deeply, and no one will cross that line.*

I couldn't help but smile softly, feeling a deep sense of joy swell within me. It wasn't just the romantic gestures, the tender moments; it was the realization that Rudhvik's love for me was so consuming, so genuine, that it made me feel worthy. The way he accepted me without question, caressing my imperfections, made me realize that I could be loved flaws and all.

It was the first time I truly understood the depth of what love could be. It wasn't about perfection; it wasn't about grand gestures or trying to meet some ideal. It was in the quiet moments, the small gestures, and the way someone looks at you and makes you feel like you are enough, just as you are.

As Rudhvik's hand found mine again, his fingers gently brushing the back of my hand, I realized just how much he cared. He wasn't just my boyfriend; he was my protector, my partner, the one who made me feel seen, loved, and valued in ways I had never imagined before. His eyes, his touch, his every gesture it was all a constant reminder that I mattered. And for the first time in my life, I knew that I truly was loved, completely and unconditionally.

And that, above all else, was enough to make my heart swell with a happiness I never knew was possible.

Eleven

Harsh Reality

I had missed my period, and feeling the weight of uncertainty, I confided in Rudhvik about it. His immediate concern was palpable, and without hesitation, he took charge and booked an appointment with a gynecologist near our house. I went to see her, and after a thorough examination, she recommended a series of tests. During our consultation, the doctor revealed a hard truth to both of us: she explained that I was not mentally prepared for physical intimacy, and the mental block I was experiencing could potentially harm my mental health.

Rudhvik, his face clouded with confusion and worry, turned to me and asked, "Is what the doctor said true? If so, why did you even agree to something you clearly weren't ready for?"

The weight of his words hit me hard, and I took a deep breath before speaking. My voice trembled as I confessed that my past fears, insecurities, and the overwhelming fear of losing him had pushed me into doing something I wasn't truly ready for. I hadn't fully processed my emotions or the fear of intimacy, and I realized that this internal struggle had not only affected my mental state but our relationship as well. I had gone against my own will because I was afraid, and it had left me feeling emotionally unprepared.

Later that evening, when the test results came back, my world 'our world' plunged into despair. The doctor diagnosed me with thin endometrium, a condition that made it difficult for me to conceive. And even if I did manage to get pregnant, the risk of miscarriage would be incredibly high.

Hearing those words felt like my heart had been shattered, like I had lost something I didn't even fully understand I could lose. The grief was overwhelming, and it made me feel as though I had failed Rudhvik, especially knowing how much he longed for a child, a daughter. The thought of not being able to give him that broke me into pieces.

In the midst of my devastation, I turned to Rudhvik, my tears flowing freely. "I'm so sorry, Rudhvik," I sobbed. "I can't fulfill your dream of giving you a daughter. I always believed in adoption, but hearing this news... it feels like a part of me has been taken away, and I don't know how to heal it."

In my sorrow, I made a desperate decision. I handed him the ring he had given me, the symbol of our commitment, thinking that maybe I wasn't enough for him and that he deserved someone who could give him the family he desired.

The next day, Rudhvik withdrew from me completely. He wouldn't speak to me, and the silence between us felt deafening. I could feel the pain emanating from him, and it tore me apart. I cried uncontrollably, feeling like I had lost him forever. But Rudhvik, being the person he was, eventually came to me, his expression soft but determined.

With a gentle but firm look, he said, "I will take you to the best doctors. We'll figure this out together. It doesn't matter whether I can have a daughter or not. What matters is you. And I'll never give up on you."

His words, so full of love and reassurance, brought a glimmer of hope into the darkness I felt inside. In that moment, I realized that Rudhvik wasn't just there for the good moments we were in together, through the challenges too. His unwavering support, his love, and his refusal to let me go, even when I felt undeserving, made me realize that we could face anything together. And in his eyes, I was enough.

But then Rudhvik did something that touched me in a way I never expected. He looked me in the eye and said, "Don't compromise physically anymore. Not for me. I know what the doctor said about how it could harm your mental health. I want you to take care of yourself, to heal, and to work through this at your own pace. I will be here for you, no matter what."

His words were the final piece of reassurance I needed. I understood that he wasn't asking for anything more from me, not when I wasn't ready, not when it could hurt me. His love for me wasn't conditional on anything, and he wanted me to heal and overcome the mental and emotional struggles I was facing.

In that moment, I felt a deep sense of relief. Rudhvik wasn't asking me to push myself further than I could go. He was asking me to prioritize my well-being, to take care of myself. And that kind of selfless, caring, patient was exactly what I had always needed.

With his unwavering support and the promise of seeking the best treatment together, I began to hope again. The road ahead would be challenging, but I wasn't alone. We were in this together, and I would fight for us. And most importantly, I would never have to compromise for the wrong reasons again.

As the day drew to a close, the weight of the evening's events still lingered in the air. The silence between Rudhvik and me had finally softened, replaced by the gentle warmth of his unwavering presence. He kept his promise, he was by my side, offering comfort and love that I didn't think I deserved, yet it was exactly what I needed.

That night, after everything that had happened, we found ourselves alone together in the quiet of our apartment. The world outside was peaceful, but inside, we were both still navigating the storm of emotions that had shaken us. The air felt thick with unspoken words, yet I could feel the tenderness in the way he held me close, as if he were silently reassuring me that everything would be okay.

Rudhvik guided me to the couch, his hand warm against the small of my back. I sank into the plush cushions, and he settled beside me, close enough that I could feel the steady rhythm of his heartbeat. He didn't need to say anything; his presence alone was enough to make me feel safe, wrapped in the comfort of his love.

I leaned my head against his shoulder, taking in the calming scent of his cologne. It was a scent I had grown to associate with home, with peace, with everything that felt right. He placed his arm around me, his fingers gently brushing through my hair, the motion slow and soothing.

"Rudhvik," I whispered, breaking the silence that had enveloped us. I needed to say it, needed him to hear me. "Thank you. For everything. For being here, for not giving up on me."

He turned slightly, his face inches from mine. His eyes were soft, filled with the depth of his love and understanding. "I'm not going anywhere, Aadhvita. You don't have to thank me. I'm here because I want to be. You mean everything to me."

His words were a balm for my soul, and I closed my eyes, allowing myself to feel the warmth of his love radiating through every inch of my being. The weight of my fears and insecurities began to lift, replaced by a quiet sense of trust and safety.

Without another word, Rudhvik tilted my chin up gently, his thumb brushing against my cheek. His touch was electric, yet tender each movement deliberate, as if he were carefully navigating the spaces between us. I could feel the air between us shift, charged with a quiet intensity that had always been there, but tonight, it was more profound than ever.

He leaned in slowly, his lips brushing against mine in a soft, lingering kiss. It wasn't just a kiss it was a promise, a reassurance that no matter what the future held, we would face it together. His lips were warm and soft, sending a rush of emotions through me that I could hardly contain. I kissed him back with equal softness, letting the love and tenderness between us speak louder than words ever could.

As we pulled back, his forehead rested gently against mine. "Aadhvita," he murmured, his voice low and full of emotion, "I want you to know that whatever happens, I'm here for you. We don't need to rush anything. We have all the time in the world."

The sincerity in his words washed over me, and I felt a sense of peace settle deep within me. I had always feared that my own insecurities and limitations would be too much for anyone to bear, but with Rudhvik, I realized that his love was not just unconditional, it was patient, kind, and unwavering.

The night stretched on, and we stayed close, allowing the quiet moments to fill the spaces between us. Rudhvik held me as I drifted off to sleep in his arms, the steady rise and fall of his chest a comforting rhythm. In that peaceful embrace, I felt the weight of the world slip away, leaving only love and trust in its place.

As the darkness of the night wrapped around us, I finally allowed myself to believe that no matter the challenges, no matter the fears or insecurities I carried, we would be okay. With Rudhvik by my side, I could face anything because love, real love, was never about perfection. It was about being there for each other, through the good times and the bad. And in that moment, with him holding me close, I knew that I had everything I ever needed.

Twelve

Strain of Separation

Rudhvik had left for a business trip, his absence stretching into what felt like an eternity. The apartment, once filled with the warmth of his presence, now felt cold, echoing with the silence he left behind. Every corner seemed to be reminding me of his absence, and I couldn't help but feel the heaviness of loneliness closing in. The quiet seemed to stretch forever, every passing minute weighed down with the pain of missing him. The longer he was away, the more restless I became, as if I was struggling to breathe in a room that had become too small.

Even in the midst of his busy schedule, Rudhvik made sure to send me little messages to remind me that he was thinking of me, and that he cared. There were phone calls late into the night, where he would pause in the middle of a hectic day just to hear my voice, to check on me. His efforts, though brief, were enough to remind me that I was never truly alone, even though his physical presence was missing. But despite his thoughtfulness, it didn't stop the ache in my chest, the yearning for him that seemed to grow each day.

One evening, the isolation was unbearable, and I couldn't fight the restlessness any longer. I needed to fill the emptiness in some way, even if only for a moment. Nirav, a close friend, had been texting me, so I decided to meet him for a drink. I just needed to get out, to escape the constant reminder of Rudhvik's absence. We found a quiet bar, the dim lighting offering a temporary escape from the thoughts clouding my mind. I ordered whiskey, the warmth of the liquid giving me a momentary sense of relief from the growing ache in my heart.

As the night went on, Nirav leaned back in his chair, a knowing smile on his face. "You know," he said softly, his gaze thoughtful, "it's clear how much you love Rudhvik."

I froze, the words catching me off guard. "What do you mean?"

He looked at me with kind eyes, as though he could see through me. "You talk about him all the time. Everything you say leads back to him. It's like he's your whole world."

I felt my heart swell at his words. There was no denying that Rudhvik was everything to me. I looked down at my drink, feeling the weight of my emotions rise. "I do love him," I admitted, my voice barely above a whisper. "More than I ever thought I could love anyone."

Nirav smiled, his voice warm with sincerity. "It's beautiful, Aadhvita. You're lucky to have that kind of love. I hope you both stay together forever. You deserve that kind of happiness."

His words, though comforting, only deepened the sense of longing I had for Rudhvik. I was desperate to hear him again, to feel that connection. As the evening went on, I found myself drinking more, the alcohol offering a numbing balm to the ache in my chest. I didn't even notice how much I had consumed until it was too late.

My phone buzzed, and I saw a message from Rudhvik. Just a simple text, asking how my evening was going. I felt a surge of emotion as I read it, and without thinking clearly, I typed back, "Out with Nirav. Having fun."

A few minutes later, my phone rang. I saw Rudhvik's name flash on the screen. My heart leapt, but as soon as I answered, I could hear the edge in his voice.

"What are you doing out this late, Aadhvita? Why are you drinking with Nirav?" he asked, his tone laced with frustration.

I was taken aback by the sharpness of his words. "Rudhvik, it's nothing," I tried to explain, my words slurring slightly. "I'm just having a drink with a friend."

"You don't get it, do you?" His voice grew more intense. "You're out drinking with a guy at this hour, and you're telling me it's nothing? It's disrespectful. I trusted you."

My chest tightened, and I felt my throat close up. His words felt like daggers, piercing through my defenses. "What do you mean, trusted me?" I asked, my own anger rising. "It's just a drink. There's nothing wrong with it."

"No, you don't understand," he said, his voice rising in anger and hurt. "I don't know if you just got drunk, or if you got close to him. I don't know if you're being honest with me anymore."

His words struck me like a punch in the gut. I felt my world begin to collapse, as though the foundation of everything we had built was crumbling before me. "Rudhvik, please," I whispered, my voice trembling. "You're overreacting."

"No, I'm not," he said bitterly. "I regret not leaving you after what happened with Dhruva. I should have known better. You've broken my trust, and I don't know if I can ever trust you again."

His words hit like a ton of bricks. I felt like I was suffocating, the air thick with the weight of the accusations. It was as if he was tearing apart the very core of who I was, making me question everything I thought I knew about myself. "Rudhvik, please," I begged, my voice breaking. "I didn't mean to hurt you."

But he was relentless, the anger in his voice building as he continued. "I don't think I can do this anymore, Aadhvita. I'm done. I'm breaking up with you."

The words were a knife to my heart. My chest constricted, and I felt as though I was being torn in two. I couldn't breathe, couldn't think. All I could do was beg, my voice barely audible, "Please, Rudhvik, don't say that. Please don't leave me."

But he was already too far gone. His decision had been made, and the finality in his words broke me. "I can't, Aadhvita. I just... can't anymore."

The phone call ended, and I was left with nothing but the deafening silence of the room, the world spinning around me. The realization that I might lose him felt like a crushing weight on my chest. I had compromised everything for him, and now it seemed like it wasn't enough. My heart shattered into a million pieces.

The next morning, I woke to the sound of the door opening. I hadn't expected Rudhvik to come home, not after what had happened the night before. But there he was, standing in the doorway, his face a mask of exhaustion and regret. His eyes were heavy, filled with the weight of the previous night's events.

"I shouldn't have said that," he mumbled, his voice thick with alcohol. "I was angry, Aadhvita. I didn't mean it."

I wanted to believe him. I wanted to hold on to his words, but the hurt still lingered, raw and fresh. "Why did you go so far, Rudhvik?" I whispered, the tears welling up in my eyes. "Why did you hurt me like that?"

He stumbled forward, collapsing onto the couch, his face buried in his hands. "I was scared, Aadhvita," he said, his voice breaking. "I didn't know what to do. I just... I didn't want to lose you. But I hurt you, and I'm sorry."

The apology came too late, and the wound was too deep. But as I sat beside him, my heart heavy with regret, I couldn't help but feel a flicker of hope. I knew that healing wouldn't be easy, but real love had the power to heal even the deepest scars. It was just going to take time, trust, and a lot of effort. And somehow, I knew that if we could survive this, we could survive anything.

As the days dragged on, the aftermath of what had happened between Rudhvik and me hung heavily in the air, Smothering and unrelenting. Every time I closed my eyes, his angry words reverberated in my mind "I'm done. I'm breaking up with you." The finality in his voice haunted me, gnawing away at my heart. It felt as though I was slowly losing the one person who had once been my everything.

I begged him. I had sacrificed my dignity, my self-worth, desperately trying to salvage something that was slipping out of my grasp. I had pleaded with him, hoping to undo the damage, to make him understand that I never intended to hurt him. But in doing so, I lost a part of myself something that couldn't be reclaimed, no matter how desperately I wished for it.

The most painful part was that I hadn't done anything wrong. I hadn't betrayed him or disrespected him in the ways he thought. Yet, in his eyes, I had become someone unworthy of his trust, someone who couldn't even be honest. His words, full of suspicion and accusation, tore through me, stripping away my confidence, my sense of self. I felt insignificant. I felt weak. I felt utterly shattered. I had given everything to hold onto us, but in the process, I had lost who I was.

Every day, I tried to move forward, pretending to be fine, but the emptiness inside me was overwhelming. I would catch glimpses of myself in the mirror and barely recognize the person staring back. I wasn't the same woman who had entered this relationship confident, hopeful, and independent. Now, I was a fragile shadow of that person, caught in a painful limbo, torn between the love I had for Rudhvik and the emotional damage that had been done.

Rudhvik, for his part, was devastated. He couldn't stand the pain he had caused me. I could see the guilt weighing him down in every gesture, every word he spoke. He regretted what he had said, and the remorse in his eyes was evident. But still, the damage had been done. His harsh words couldn't be undone with apologies alone.

One evening, after days of silence, he came to me, his face etched with pain.

"I'm so sorry, Aadhvita," he said quietly, his voice thick with emotion. "I shouldn't have said those things. I regret it with all my heart. I hurt you, and I can never take it back."

His apology was heartfelt, and for a moment, it nearly broke me to see him so vulnerable. But even as he spoke, I knew the truth: his words, his accusations, had cut me so deeply that they could never be erased. It wasn't just about the argument or the alcohol. It was about the trust that had been shattered, the respect lost, and the emotional toll it had taken on me.

He knelt before me, his face desperate, pleading. "Please, Aadhvita. I love you. I don't want to lose you. Please don't let this be the end of us."

Tears welled in his eyes, and I could feel the rawness of his regret. For a moment, I almost believed we could go back to how things were before, but deep inside, I knew it wasn't that simple. Trust had been broken, and healing wasn't something that could happen overnight. His apology, though genuine, couldn't undo the emotional damage he had caused me.

"I want to forgive you, Rudhvik," I whispered, my voice barely audible. "But I can't forget how you made me feel. I lost a part of myself that night. I begged you,

I gave up my self-respect... for love. And now, I don't even recognize who I am anymore. It hurts. It hurts more than I ever thought possible."

His hand trembled as he reached for mine. "I know, Aadhvita. I know. And I'll spend my life making this right. Please, don't give up on us."

His words, filled with desperation, tugged at my heart, but the truth remained I couldn't heal just because he was sorry. The damage had been done, and I didn't know how to fix it. Love wasn't enough to erase the hurt.

"I don't know if I can trust you again, Rudhvik," I said, my voice breaking. "I don't know if I can love you the same way anymore."

His face crumbled as the tears flowed freely. "I'll do whatever it takes, Aadhvita. I'll be patient. I'll give you all the time you need. I'll never stop fighting for us."

I wanted to believe him. I wanted to believe that, in time, we could rebuild what had been broken. But deep down, I knew that I had to find myself again before I could truly give him my heart. I wasn't sure when or how that would happen, but I understood that healing required more than just words. It required time, patience, and a rebuilding of trust, a trust that had been shattered by a single night of misunderstanding.

For now, I could only hope that, with time, the wounds would begin to heal. I could only hope that, eventually,

I would be able to forgive him completely, without the weight of my insecurities and pain. That maybe, one day, we could be stronger for all we had endured.

But, for now, the ache lingered, a constant reminder that love, no matter how deep, could hurt in ways that no one could prepare for. And healing wasn't something that could be rushed. It was something we both needed to fight for together or apart. Only time would tell if we could Surmount it.

Thirteen

A Secret Vow

The weight of the past was becoming unbearable. It felt like each day, the insecurity, fear, and the crippling anxiety of losing Rudhvik were slowly eroding my peace. The haunting shadows of past wounds, which had long been buried, resurfaced, clawing at me with a sharpness that I could no longer ignore. I feared the worst, especially with him being away for work, and the thought of him slipping away from me made my heart ache with a desperation I couldn't control. It was as if my whole world was held together by the thinnest thread, and every time he wasn't around, that thread frayed a little more.

One evening, overwhelmed by my own emotions, I could no longer hold it in. The anxiety was too much, and the fear of losing him threatened to consume me. I looked at Rudhvik, my heart pounding in my chest, and I let the words escape before I even had time to stop myself. "I want to marry you, Rudhvik," I said, my voice trembling with vulnerability. The declaration felt like a raw, exposed truth, one that had lived deep inside of me but had never been spoken aloud. In that moment, it felt as if all my fears and insecurities faded away, replaced by something real: a longing for permanence, a longing to belong to him forever.

Rudhvik didn't say anything immediately. He just held my gaze, the quiet understanding between us almost palpable. His eyes softened, and I could tell he had sensed the weight of my confession, the depth of my longing.

Later that evening, as I was in the kitchen, busy preparing a surprise dinner for him, something unexpected happened. I had been so caught up in the preparations, trying to perfect every dish, that I didn't even hear the door open. When I turned around, there he was standing in the doorway, a small box in his hand. The look on his face was one I couldn't quite place, but there was something gentle and knowing in his eyes.

He stepped forward, placing the box in my hands. "I have something for you," he said quietly, his voice filled with the weight of unspoken emotion. I opened the box, and inside was a beautiful pendant with a delicate heart with a key nestled within it. The silver gleamed softly under the dim light, and as I traced the intricate design with my fingers, my heart fluttered in my chest.

"Rudhvik, it's beautiful," I whispered, the words almost escaping me in a daze.

He took the pendant from the box and, without a word, gently lifted it to my neck. His fingers brushed against my skin as he fastened the clasp, and in that quiet, intimate moment, he spoke the words that would forever stay with me. "We are now married, Aadhvita. This pendant is a symbol of our togetherness, a promise that we'll always be inseparable, no matter what comes our way. I'm giving you this not as a gift, but as a symbol of my commitment to you, to us."

His voice was steady, but I could see the vulnerability in his eyes, the love and sincerity that radiated from him. I felt a rush of warmth spread through me, the overwhelming joy of knowing he felt as deeply for me as I did for him. I could barely contain my emotions, and a tear slipped down my cheek, but this time, it wasn't from sorrow. It was from an overwhelming feeling of being loved in a way I had always dreamed of.

I touched the pendant gently, my heart full. "I vow, Rudhvik," I said, my voice shaky with emotion, "I will love you with all my heart. And I promise, I'll be the best partner I can be for you. You've shown me a love I didn't think was possible, and I'll never take it for granted."

He smiled softly, pulling me into his arms. "You already are," he whispered, holding me close. "And I promise, I will be the best husband ever. Always."

There was something so profound in that moment, something that made me feel like everything was finally falling into place. His love, his commitment, his presence was all I had ever wanted, and now it was mine. It felt as if the years of uncertainty and fear had led to this single, perfect moment of clarity.

That night, as the world outside seemed to fade away, we decided to take the next step in our relationship, not just physically, but emotionally. It wasn't just about intimacy it was about solidifying the bond that we had worked so hard to build. It was about sealing our promises, knowing that this was the beginning of a deeper connection.

As we shared the night together, it felt like our hearts and souls were entwined in a way that no words could fully capture. Each touch, each kiss, each whispered word was a vow in itself, reaffirming our commitment to one another. It wasn't just passion, it was the embodiment of everything we had shared, everything we had overcome, and everything we hoped to build together.

When the night finally settled into silence, I lay next to him, my heart racing with the intensity of the love we shared. The fears, the insecurities, and the anxiety of the past seemed to evaporate in the glow of our bond. We were no longer just two people sharing a life, we were a team, a unit, bound together by love and a promise that nothing could break.

"I love you, Rudhvik," I whispered as I rested my head on his chest.

"I love you too, Aadhvita. Always."

At that moment, I knew that no matter what the future held, we would face it together. We had sealed our commitment not just with a pendant, but with the unbreakable bond that had grown between us over time. And as we drifted to sleep in each other's arms, I knew our love had reached a new, unshakable level. This was just the beginning, and together, we could face anything that came our way.

Fourteen

Ripping the Soul

The evening began with a sense of anticipation, fueled by hope, a kind of hope that only comes from a love so strong it feels unbreakable. Rudhvik had been planning for this night, a family dinner at our cozy apartment. Everything had been set up perfectly. The table was laid out with care, and the air was filled with the delightful aroma of the meal he had lovingly prepared. The warm glow of the lights softened the room, but despite all the effort and thought that went into it, I couldn't shake the anxiety gripping my chest. This was the night where everything could change.

Rudhvik had been so confident about the evening, but I was filled with dread. I knew how strict my father was about family and traditions. The thought of confronting him about marrying Rudhvik someone from a different caste terrified me. In my mind, it seemed like an impossible conversation, one I wasn't sure I could initiate. I had spent years avoiding it, convincing myself that somehow, the moment would never come. But here we were, on the brink of a conversation that could shatter everything.

When my parents arrived, the weight of the moment settled heavily upon me. My heart pounded in my chest, and I could feel the cold sweat on my palms. I greeted them as best I could, trying to mask my anxiety, but my mom's unchanging face and my dad's stern silence only made it worse. We all sat down at the table, trying to make small talk, but it felt like there was a heavy cloud hanging over the room. The awkwardness was palpable, and every word spoken felt like it could either make things better or make them infinitely worse.

Rudhvik sat next to me, but the distance between us felt miles apart. I could feel his gaze on me, waiting, urging me to be the one to break the silence. But I couldn't. I wasn't ready. My fear, my years of conditioning, had gripped me too tightly.

Then, after what felt like an eternity, Rudhvik took the lead. He cleared his throat, his eyes meeting mine for a brief moment, as if silently asking for my permission to speak. I could see the determination in his eyes, the love he had for me, and the courage he was mustering to take this step. "I need to say something," he said, turning toward my parents.

The room fell silent, and the air seemed to freeze. My heart raced in my chest as I tried to brace myself for what was coming. "I love Aadhvita," Rudhvik continued, his voice steady but filled with emotion. "And I want to marry her. We've been through so much together, and I believe it's time we move forward. We're ready for the next step."

I could see my mother's face harden, her lips pressing into a thin line. I wanted to say something to tell her how much he meant to me but the words caught in my throat. My father's gaze darkened, his lips pulling back in a tight frown. I felt like the walls were closing in around me, and for a moment, I couldn't breathe. The air felt heavy, stifling, like I was suffocating under the pressure.

"Father, please," I finally spoke, my voice trembling. "I love him. We've been together for years now. Please understand."

But my father was unmoved. His voice was cold, final. "This is not how things are done. Intercaste marriage is unacceptable in this family. You know that."

The weight of his words crushed me. I had known this moment would come, but hearing it, hearing him say it out loud, felt like a blow to the heart. I looked at Rudhvik, and I saw the hurt in his eyes. He had hoped for a different outcome, but it was clear that this was the reality we were facing.

I tried to hold back my tears, but they were threatening to spill over. "Dad, please," I whispered, my voice cracking. "Please don't say that."

But it was too late. My father's mind was made up. His gaze was hard and unwavering. "I won't allow it. This is not negotiable."

I felt myself go numb, the anger and heartbreak welling up inside me, but I couldn't even find the strength to speak. The disappointment in my mother's eyes was the final blow. She stood up without a word, her face cold and indifferent. "We're leaving," she said, her voice lacking any emotion.

My father followed her out of the apartment, leaving me standing there, paralyzed. I couldn't move, couldn't speak. All I could hear was the sound of their footsteps echoing in my mind. The dinner we had carefully planned, the hope we had invested in this evening, had been shattered in an instant.

Rudhvik's parents, who had been so kind and hopeful just moments ago, now sat in stunned silence, unsure of what to say or do. I turned to Rudhvik, my heart aching for him, for us, but the words I wanted to say caught in my throat. What could I say? How could I explain this? The truth was, I couldn't change my parents' mind. I couldn't bridge the gap that had always existed between us.

Without another word, I broke down. Tears streamed down my face as I collapsed onto the couch, my body shaking uncontrollably. Rudhvik knelt beside me, his hands trembling as he reached for mine. "I'm sorry," he whispered, his voice cracking. "I never meant for this to happen. I thought we could do it together."

His words only made the pain worse, and I pulled away, burying my face in my hands. "I couldn't do it. I couldn't convince them," I sobbed, the guilt and sorrow washing over me like a tidal wave.

Rudhvik's face twisted in pain. He sat beside me, his arm around me, but there was a cold distance between us now. I could see it in his eyes—he was crushed. His love for me was strong, but he was tired of waiting. He was tired of seeing me trapped between my family's expectations and my love for him.

"You need to be the one to make this decision," he said quietly, his voice heavy with disappointment. "If you can't convince your parents, if you can't fight for us... then I don't know if I can keep waiting. I can't let our families down, Aadhvita. I just can't."

His words were a punch to my gut. I had failed him. I had failed us. And in that moment, I realized that we were standing on the precipice of something far more painful than I had imagined.

"I can't... I don't know what to do," I whispered, my heart breaking.

Rudhvik stood up slowly, his back turned to me as he grabbed his coat. "I need time, Aadhvita. I need to go back to my hometown. I can't keep going like this. If you can't fight for us, if you can't convince your parents..." His voice trailed off, filled with uncertainty and hurt. "I just... I can't do this anymore."

The words hit me like a cold slap. I had lost him, hadn't I? My fear and hesitation had cost me everything. As Rudhvik walked toward the door, I wanted to scream, to beg him to stay, but I was frozen, paralyzed by my own regret.

And as he left, I realized that I was standing at the crossroads of a future I wasn't sure I could have, a love I wasn't sure I could keep. The pain of rejection from my family, coupled with the loss of Rudhvik's trust, felt like a wound that might never heal.

Rudhvik walked out that evening without looking back, and I stood frozen, unable to do anything but watch him go. He hadn't wanted to leave, I knew that. He had been torn, his eyes filled with pain as he quietly gathered his things. But he was a man bound by family expectations, his own pride, his responsibilities to his parents. And in the end, it wasn't just about us anymore. It was about the weight of his own family's demands. He couldn't bear the thought of disappointing them, even if it meant walking away from everything he and I had built together.

I never thought that would be the last time I'd see him for so long. The door clicked shut behind him, and I collapsed onto the couch, the silence of the apartment swallowing me whole. My tears fell freely, mixing with the realization that something had broken that couldn't be fixed. He had made the choice he prioritized his family over us. And even though I understood his position, the hurt was undeniable.

Days passed, but there was no call, no message, not a single attempt from him to reach out. I thought maybe, just maybe, he would come back. He would show up at my door, ready to fight for us, ready to convince my parents that we could be happy together, despite everything. I told myself it was just a matter of time. He would make the effort. I had given him time and space, sure he would do what he had always done, take the lead, fight for us, make the decision that we both needed. But nothing came.

I waited, day after day, staring at my phone, checking it again and again, hoping for a message, a call, something. But nothing. The silence between us was deafening, and I started to question myself. Was I waiting for something that would never come? Was I fooling myself into believing that he would come back?

Eventually, I couldn't take it anymore. I thought about what he had said before he left, that I needed to talk to my parents first. He needed me to initiate, to open the door, to break the silence. He would try to convince them after I made that first step, he had promised. But deep down, I knew that was never going to happen. I knew my parents, the unyielding strength of their traditions, the strictness of their beliefs. No matter how much I loved him, no matter how hard I tried, they would never accept someone like Rudhvik. Not because of who he was as a person, but because of the caste divide, because of everything that had been ingrained in them, everything they had held onto for generations.

I couldn't bring myself to call him. I couldn't bring myself to face that reality, to admit that all my hopes for the future had been dashed by the weight of something I couldn't control. He had walked away, and I had let him.

Days turned into weeks, and the distance between us grew like a chasm I couldn't cross. I kept telling myself I would reach out, but every time I picked up my phone, I hesitated. What would I say? That I was still waiting for him to come back, to convince my parents? What if he had already moved on? What if I had misread everything between us? The uncertainty gnawed at me, but the thought of facing my parents again, after all this, terrified me.

I began to realize that maybe he wasn't coming back. Maybe he had chosen his family, as I feared he would. And in that realization, the pain cut deeper.

As time passed, I felt a growing emptiness inside. I had always been the one who feared being abandoned, the one who couldn't bear to face rejection. But now, it was happening in the most painful way possible not because Rudhvik had decided to leave me outright, but because he had given up on us without a fight.

I wasn't sure how much more of this I could take. Would he ever reach out? Would he ever come back and tell me that he had fought for us, that he had tried to change my parents' minds? Or was I just another chapter in his life that he had closed without looking back?

The silence that followed felt heavier than anything. And in that silence, I was left wondering if the love we shared was strong enough to survive the weight of family and tradition or if, like everything else in my life, it had simply faded away without me ever being able to hold on to it.

After few days

The sun had just begun to set that evening, casting a soft golden light through my apartment windows as I sat lost in my thoughts, trying to make sense of everything that had happened. The silence between Rudhvik and me had become unbearable, and the unanswered questions in my mind consumed me. I had spent days replaying everything in my head, wondering if there was a way back, if there was still a chance for us. I kept convincing myself that somehow, things would work out, that we could fix it somehow.

Then, my phone buzzed, interrupting the silence. My heart skipped a beat as I saw Rudhvik's name on the screen. I quickly unlocked my phone, almost afraid to read the message, not knowing what to expect. As my eyes skimmed the words on the screen, they seemed to blur together at first, but with each line, the cold reality set in, and the weight of his words hit me like a punch to the gut.

"I love you, Aadhvita, but your fear led us to a separation that I can't undo. If you will not tell your parents about us, how will I go and introduce my parents to them and ask for your hand in marriage? You know I can't go against my parents, Aadhvita. Separation is the only way left for us now. If not in this lifetime, then maybe in the next lifetime, we'll be together."

His words echoed in my mind, each one more suffocating than the last. I sat there, staring at the screen, unable to process the enormity of what he had said. The weight of his decision crushed me. *Separation is the only way left for us* that phrase played in my head over and over again. And with it, a cold realization crept in: he had given up. He had walked away, leaving me with nothing but the ghost of our love.

The pain that followed was indescribable. For the first time in years, I felt completely empty, as if I had no purpose, no reason to keep moving forward. My chest tightened, and the suffocating feeling of despair settled deep within me. I had always feared this moment, the moment when love wasn't enough, when circumstances, tradition, and family would tear us apart. And now it has happened. He was gone, and there was nothing left for me in the city that had once felt like home.

For the next three days, I didn't eat, didn't speak. I couldn't bring myself to leave my apartment, couldn't find the strength to face the world. I had fallen into a kind of numbness, a painful void where every thought and emotion felt too heavy to carry. I couldn't stop thinking about the finality of his message. It felt like I had lost everything, the love I thought would last forever, the future I had imagined with him, the hope I had clung to.

And then, as the days dragged on in a haze of sorrow, a decision began to form within me, slowly but surely. I realized that staying in this city, with these memories, was only suffocating me further. I needed to leave. I needed to go somewhere where I could heal, where I could find solace. I needed my mother, her embrace, her comforting words. I needed the warmth of her presence more than ever.

And so, I made the decision. I would leave. I would return home to my mother's arms, to the place where I had once felt safe and loved. Maybe, just maybe, being there would help me find some sense of peace, some way to mend the broken pieces of myself. The city that had once felt like a new beginning now felt like a prison, a place filled with memories of a love that was lost.

As I packed my things, the weight of it all settled on my shoulders. Leaving felt like the only choice left for me. I had tried everything to make things work with Rudhvik, but now, all I had left were the broken shards of a dream that would never come true. The hope of a future with him was now a distant memory, something I would have to let go of no matter how much it hurt.

I caught a glimpse of myself in the mirror as I finished packing. I didn't recognize the person staring back at me. She looked lost, broken, as if the light had been extinguished from her eyes. But somewhere deep inside, I knew I had to keep going. I had to return to where it all began, to where I could find the strength to heal.

With one last glance at the apartment, I left, the door clicking shut behind me with a finality that echoed in my chest. I had nothing left here. It was time to go back home, to seek comfort in the arms of the one person who had always been there for me, my mother. Maybe there, I could start to rebuild myself, piece by piece, until one day, the pain would fade.

But for now, I had nothing but the open road ahead of me, and the hope that somehow, someday, I would find peace again.

I arrived at my childhood home in Indore, a city that immediately embraced me with its familiar charm and peaceful atmosphere. The vintage duplex, with its blend of traditional architecture and semi-modern touches, offered a sense of comfort I had long missed. The wooden floors creaked beneath me as I walked through the spacious, high-ceilinged rooms adorned with antique tapestries and family photographs. The warm, golden light streaming through the large windows illuminated the rustic furniture, while the old wooden fortune in the corner reminded me of my family's rich history. The kitchen smelled of my mother's cooking, and my childhood room felt like a comforting sanctuary. In this cozy, familiar space, I found solace from the pain of the past, feeling at home once more amidst the timeless embrace of the house.

The first thing I did when I stepped inside was rush to my mother, who greeted me with a warm, comforting embrace. Her once-dark hair now had streaks of grey, but she still radiated the same softness and beauty she always had, with a quiet elegance shaped by time and life's experiences. Her skin, delicate as cotton, carried the traces of age but also a wisdom that gave her a serene and undefinable beauty. As she held me, I felt an overwhelming sense of peace, as though the world's burdens could momentarily be lifted. She was seated in the balcony, immersed in the Autobiography *of a Yogi* by Paramahansa Yogananda. Watching her, I felt a surge of strength, knowing that if I had her by my side, I could survive.

I wrapped my arms around my mother, holding her close, and she responded instantly, her embrace warm and reassuring, like a balm to my wounded heart. Her face lit up with joy at my presence, as if the world was right again. She quickly went to the kitchen, preparing my favorite dish, something so comforting and familiar that it felt like the years of separation never existed. We sat together, sharing laughs and stories, the warmth of family filling the space that had once felt so empty.

But eventually, the weight of everything I'd been carrying overwhelmed me. As the evening settled, I opened up to her, sharing every detail of the pain I had endured, of how much I loved Rudhvik and the heartbreak of our separation.

She listened quietly, her expression serious. When I finished, she took a deep breath, her eyes filled with a mixture of concern and understanding. "No one in our family will ever accept your relationship, Aadhvita," she said softly, her words cutting through me like a sharp weapon. "You need to understand that and move on. Time will heal you. It will heal both of you. Rudhvik will move on, too."

Her words pierced me deeply, a hollow ache spreading through my chest. I couldn't bring myself to argue or explain to her how impossible that seemed. I couldn't tell her that I felt like I was left with nothing, that Rudhvik was my entire world, the very air I breathed. He had my soul, not just my body. He was everything I had ever wanted, and I couldn't fathom a future without him in it.

But all I could do was nod, swallowing the bitter reality. According to my family and many others around the world, time would heal everything. I was meant to move on. So, I left everything in time's hands, even though a part of me died inside with every passing day that I couldn't reach out to him, couldn't be with him. And I knew, deep down, that this time apart would either heal me or tear me apart completely.

Fifteen

Stepping Into Something Eternal

It's been so long, and I'm still trying to heal though, if I'm honest, I haven't really tried. I've almost grown accustomed to the emptiness that fills the spaces he once occupied in my heart. I started visiting a nearby orphanage regularly, trying to find something to fill the void, something that could bring meaning back into my life. One day, during my visit, I met a little girl whose eyes seemed to carry a story of their own. She had a small birthmark just above her left eye, right where her eyelashes met the skin, a mark that struck me instantly. It was so familiar. It reminded me of Rudhvik, who had a similar scar, though I never knew where it came from.

In that moment, everything shifted. I felt a connection so deep, so immediate, it was as though the universe was telling me this was my purpose. I remembered how eagerly Rudhvik had talked about wanting a daughter, a daughter he could raise to be strong and courageous, someone who would defy all the taboos and expectations of the world. I knew, in my heart, that I had to adopt this little girl. It wasn't an easy decision, though. I was single, and my parents had always expected me to marry something I wasn't ready for.

For a month, I tried to convince my parents, lying about not being fit for marriage, telling them that my future was with this daughter I intended to adopt. It was a difficult, uncomfortable truth to sell, but somehow, they agreed. My father, although skeptical at first, eventually supported me and helped with the legal process. That process took almost a year, but in the end, I adopted Navika. I welcomed her into my life with a grand celebration, the kind of joy I thought I'd never feel again.

Every little step she takes, every milestone she reaches, reminds me of Rudhvik. She's my reflection of him, her stubbornness, her unwavering commitment, the way she values every single moment with me. Her presence brings me peace, and in some way, her habits mirror the very things that made Rudhvik who he was the man who was once my world.

My family embraced Navika as one of their own. They love her like she is my biological child, which, in a way, she is. My life with Navika has become easier, more fulfilling, and brighter in ways I didn't think possible. Yet, there's still that part of me that aches, wondering if Rudhvik has moved on if someone else has taken the place he once had in my heart. The thought of him belonging to someone else, of him loving someone else, cuts through me, leaving me raw.

I wish he had made that last effort, the one I couldn't summon the courage for—to speak to my parents, to fight for us. But instead, I've learned to accept the life I've chosen. I've compromised my everything for my love for him, and I don't regret it. I'll celebrate every memory of Rudhvik through my daughter, Navika, his reflection in her every laugh, every gesture, every stubborn moment. She carries a piece of him with her, and that's enough.

As for healing, I've realized it's something I'll never truly experience. The memories of him will always remain, etched deep within me, sealed forever. But as long as I have Navika, his presence lingers in a way that helps me carry on. And maybe, that's the closest I'll ever come to healing.

Sixteen

'Forever Intertwined'

This is the story of my heart. When it beats, it's not just for me it's for her. She's the reason I never gave up. Every time I tried to fall apart, she was there, making me stronger with more love in her heart. Even after I hurt her with my harsh words, even after I tore at her with my actions, she came back with a resolve stronger than before, but there are moments in life when you encounter someone who doesn't just change you, but elevates you to a place you didn't even know you could reach. For me, that person is Aadhvita.

From the first time I met her, I felt a deep connection, as though her spirit and mine were meant to intertwine. She was different not just because of her beauty, but because of the way she carried herself, the way she loved so effortlessly. Every day she showed me that love wasn't just an emotion but a force that could build, heal, and empower.

Her love became the foundation of everything I believed in. She wasn't someone who just made me feel special, but someone who made me believe in the best version of myself. With her, I found a strength and a joy I had never known. Her laughter, her unwavering belief in us, and her boundless compassion lifted me to heights I hadn't imagined. She became the brightness I had always searched for, and every day with her was a reminder of the love we shared.

Through all of it, Aadhvita showed me that love is not passive; it's transformative. Every time we faced challenges, she never wavered. She gave with a heart full of trust and kindness, and in doing so, she opened doors in me I had never thought to walk through. Her presence was a healing touch, not because I was broken, but because she knew how to bring out the fullness of who I was.

The true depth of Aadhvita's love was revealed in her sacrifices, those moments when she put aside her own needs, her own desires, to create something meaningful between us. She gave of herself, not because she felt she had to, but because she understood the importance of building a life rooted in trust, understanding, and mutual respect.

There were times when I saw her give up parts of herself to support me, to support us. She never asked for anything in return, except for my commitment, my heart, and my trust. And in the most selfless act, she adopted a daughter, Navika, an act of love that extended far beyond her own needs. It wasn't just about creating a family for herself; it was about building a future for both of us, even when I didn't fully grasp it.

She never once lost sight of the love she held for me, even in moments where I struggled to find the words to show her how deeply I cared. Her capacity for love was unmatched, and it inspired me to be better, to strive for more. In every way, she taught me the true meaning of love, that is no less than a devotion not as a burden, but as a choice made from a place of deep love and understanding.

Her sacrifices were not out of weakness but were a testament to her incredible strength. She never expected me to fix everything, but she showed me how love could be an anchor through even the most uncertain times. She believed in us, in a future that was bright and full of potential, and in doing so, she gave me the courage to believe in that future too.

Ultimately, the time came when we both had to make a choice. Our love was undeniable, but we recognized that our paths needed to diverge in order for both of us to grow. I thought that by stepping back, by allowing space between us, I was giving her the opportunity to heal, to release the fears and insecurities that had kept her from fully embracing all that we could be together. I mistakenly believed that by letting her go, she would find the freedom she needed to heal completely and one day release all her fears and insecurities. But in doing so, I hurt her more than I ever intended. My hope was that she would find her own strength, but in reality, I had misunderstood what she needed.

What I failed to realize was that her healing didn't require me to distance myself from her. Her strength wasn't something I needed to push her toward by creating space, it was something she had been showing me all along. She had already given so much of herself for us, for our future, and my decision to let go wasn't an act of love. It was a misstep, an attempt to fix something that wasn't broken, to give her space when what she truly needed was my unwavering support and presence.

She chose a path that would allow her to grow, not because she didn't love me, but because she understood that our love had to take different forms. She chose to focus on her own journey, to embrace her purpose, and in doing so, she showed me the real depth of love, one that was not bound by need or fear, but by strength and wisdom.

In the end, I see now that her decision was not about letting go, but about trusting that love, even when it is challenged, will always find its way. She chose love not as a possession to hold onto, but as a gift that would carry us both forward, no matter where life took us.

Though we walk different paths now, I know that our souls are forever intertwined, and one day, they will reunite. I have no doubt that in whatever form our love takes, it will endure. Aadhvita's love has already won because it is timeless, selfless, and eternal. Her love isn't defined by possession or control; it is free, powerful, and unyielding. And that is how I know that we are meant to find each other again, when the time is right.